"Who is the woman sitting opposite me now?" Massimo asked. "Is she the social-climbing gold digger, or the girl with the golden heart?"

"What if I am both?" she asked, a fleeting shadow of sadness in her gray-blue eyes as they returned to his. "What if they are one and the same?"

The waiter appeared at that moment to take their order, giving Massimo time to reflect on her answer. Massimo had waited so long for revenge. He had thought of nothing else for five long years. Each punishing day working at building his investment empire had been for this chance to turn the tables on her. He had been ruthless in his pursuit of wealth and power. His anger toward his stepfather had become almost insignificant as he had planned his revenge on her.

He was not going to be lured in by her innocent act all over again.

This time he would have her where he wanted her, where he had dreamed of having her for the past five years.

In his bed.

MELANIE MILBURNE read her first Harlequin® novel when she was seventeen and has never looked back. She decided she would settle for nothing less than a tall, dark and handsome hero as her future husband. Well, she's not only still reading romance, but writing it as well! And the tall, dark and handsome hero? She fell in love with him on the second date and was secretly engaged to him within six weeks.

Two sons later, they arrived in Hobart, Tasmania—the jewel in the Australian crown. Once their boys were safely in school, Melanie went back to university and upgraded, receiving her bachelor's and then her master's degree.

As part of her final assessment, she conducted a tutorial on the romance genre. While she was reading a paragraph from the novel of a prominent Harlequin® author, the door suddenly burst open. The husband she thought was working was actually standing there dressed in a tuxedo, his dark brown eyes centered on her startled blue ones. He strode purposefully across the room, hauled Melanie into his arms and kissed her deeply and passionately before setting her back down and leaving without a single word. The lecturer gave Melanie a high distinction and her fellow students gave her jealous glares! And so her pilgrimage into romance writing was set!

Melanie also enjoys long-distance running and is a nationally ranked masters swimmer in Australia. She learned to swim as an adult, so for anyone out there who thinks they can't do something—you can! Her motto is "Don't say I can't; say I CAN TRY."

ANDROLETTI'S
MISTRESS
MELANIE MILBURNE

~ UNEXPECTED BABIES ~

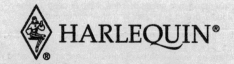

HARLEQUIN®

TORONTO • NEW YORK • LONDON
AMSTERDAM • PARIS • SYDNEY • HAMBURG
STOCKHOLM • ATHENS • TOKYO • MILAN • MADRID
PRAGUE • WARSAW • BUDAPEST • AUCKLAND

Recycling programs
for this product may
not exist in your area.

ISBN-13: 978-0-373-52713-7
ISBN-10:   0-373-52713-6

ANDROLETTI'S MISTRESS

First North American Publication 2009.

Copyright © 2007 by Melanie Milburne.

ANDROLETTI'S
MISTRESS

To my mother-in-law, Joyce, and my late father-in-law, Alf Wilkinson. I dedicate this book to you for the very special gift you gave me in producing the most adorable man in the world—your son. Thank you from the bottom of my heart. Love you.

CHAPTER ONE

IT WAS the sort of funeral where no one shed a tear.

Nikki accepted everyone's condolences with a composed expression on her face, even though in spite of everything she still felt a sense of deep sadness as the coffin was lowered into the cold, dark soil.

'So sorry about Joseph,' one of the sales managers said as he shook her hand a few minutes later. 'But he wouldn't want to have lingered on any longer.'

'Thank you, Henry,' she said, even managing to crack a small, grateful smile. 'No, indeed he wouldn't.'

'Mrs Ferliani?' A journalist pushed through the small knot of mourners. 'Have you any comment on the successful takeover bid of Ferliani Fashions conducted by your late husband's stepson Massimo Androletti?'

Nikki felt a shockwave go through her body at the mention of that name. She'd already scanned the small congregation repeatedly, in case he'd had the audacity to appear, but so far she hadn't caught sight of him. 'No, I haven't,' she said coolly. 'Now, please leave; this is a private ceremony.'

'Is it true there is nothing left of your late husband's

estate?' the journalist persisted. 'That Massimo Androletti now owns the business and even the house you live in?'

Nikki set her mouth. 'I have no comment.'

Another reporter joined the first. 'Our sources say Joseph Ferliani lost a fortune on the stock exchange, and in an effort to recoup the losses gambled away everything he and you owned.'

'Mrs Ferliani has already told you she has no comment to make,' a deep male voice said from just behind Nikki.

She swung around to look a long way upwards into the black, diamond gaze of Massimo Androletti. She fought hard not to reveal how seeing him after all this time affected her, but Nikki was almost certain he had noticed the tiny up-and-down movement of her throat. His expression was mask-like, but there was a glint of steely purpose in his eyes that secretly terrified her. Her stomach hollowed out, her legs began to tremble and her chest felt as if something hard and thick had lodged itself halfway down, making it almost impossible to draw in the air necessary to breathe.

'Come this way,' he said, putting a hand beneath her elbow, the touch of his fingers sending a current of tingling awareness right through the thick sleeve of her winter coat.

Nikki considered resisting his attempt to lead her away, but thought better of it when she felt the subtle tightening of his hold, as if he'd already sensed her intention. As she felt his latent strength, her heart began to thump behind the wall of her chest as she thought of being alone with him.

He led her to his waiting limousine parked outside the cemetery. 'Get in,' he commanded curtly. 'We have things to discuss.'

Nikki sat on the plush leather seat, her legs pressed tightly together as he joined her, the huge car now seeming far too small with his long legs and six-foot-three frame taking up most of the available space. Even the air inside the car seemed to have been reduced; it physically hurt to take in each breath as she tried to steady her growing panic with deep, calm breaths.

'To the house, thank you, Ricardo,' Massimo said as he leaned forward to speak through the panel.

Nikki shifted even further away as he sat back in the seat, her nostrils flaring slightly as the spicy fragrance of his after-shave drifted towards her. Her stomach gave a little flutter as her eyes went to the long, hard length of his thighs within touching distance of hers. She had once felt those strong legs entwined with hers, had felt his hard male body drive into her silky moistness, his hot, commanding mouth wreak havoc on all of her senses.

'So,' he said as he swung his cold, hard gaze towards her. 'Your plans to land yourself a fortune failed in the end, did they not?'

Nikki tightened her mouth without responding to his embittered jibe. He had a right to be bitter, she had to admit. She would have felt the same, if not worse, if he had done the same to her. But explaining her actions five years down the track would be pointless. Given the choice, she would have done the same thing again in spite of all it had cost her.

'It is true what the journalist said. I now own everything,' he said into the silence, which was taut as a violin bow. 'But then I expect the lawyer has already explained that to you.'

'No,' she said, stripping the one word of any trace of emotion. 'I haven't yet met with him, but I plan to do so tomorrow.'

His dark brows rose slightly. 'I would have thought that would have been your very first priority,' he said with a cynical glint in his eyes. 'A sluttish little gold-digger like you would surely check to see what has been left to her on her husband's death?'

Nikki refused to show the despair she was feeling at his comment. Instead she elevated her chin and sent him an arctic look. 'Joseph was far more important to me than his money,' she said. 'I don't care if he's left me nothing.'

His mouth tilted into a calculating smile. 'Such wifely devotion,' he drawled. 'But then you are very good at acting when it suits you, are you not?'

She turned her head away to stare sightlessly out of the window.

'He has left you nothing,' Massimo said into the strained silence. 'Nothing except debt, that is. Even the house is now mine.'

This time it was harder not to reveal how his statement affected her. She fought to control her expression, but she could feel the tensing of her jaw regardless as she turned back to glare at him. 'I don't believe you. Joseph promised he would provide for me.'

'The way I see it, you are in a rather precarious position,' he went on evenly, although his coal-black eyes still shone with hatred. 'You have no income unless I choose to give it to you, no car, no house, and as of a week ago, no sugar daddy.'

Nikki really loathed that term. It demeaned everything she had come to admire and respect in Massimo's stepfather.

Joseph Ferliani had had his faults; he had been a hard-nosed businessman for most of his life. But for all that, she had come to know him in a way she suspected few people ever had. The long, agonising months of his terminal illness had shown a side to him that he had kept well hidden, and most particularly from his stepson and arch-enemy Massimo Androletti.

'Your stepfather was not my sugar daddy,' she said in a clipped tone as she faced his obsidian gaze head-on.

His top lip lifted in disdain. 'What was he, then?'

'He was my husband and my friend,' she answered with quiet dignity.

Something flickered in his eyes at the word 'husband', for which again Nikki couldn't really blame him. It would gall most men to think they had been replaced by someone much older and richer than they were, and Massimo was clearly no different. She could feel his blistering rage in the air that separated them; her skin felt tight and prickly, and the hairs on the back of her neck lifted one by one as his eyes clashed with hers.

'You forgot to mention he was your lover,' he pointed out with another curl of his lip. 'Or did he not come up to scratch in the bedroom?'

Nikki turned away again so he wouldn't see the way her face flamed with colour. 'I don't wish to discuss my private details with you,' she said. 'It's disrespectful, considering Joseph is not even cold in his grave, and to be quite frank it's none of your business.'

'It was my business five years ago, wasn't it, Nikki?' he reminded her. 'But little did I know then that one drink would lead to a one-night stand with my stepfather's future child bride.'

She ground her teeth together and bit out, 'I was nineteen years old, surely old enough to know my own mind?'

'You went from my bed straight to his,' he said, his dark eyes flashing with livid sparks of fury.

Nikki felt her insides twisting with anguish. 'I didn't know who you were,' she said. 'Joseph never mentioned your name to me prior to our…marriage.'

'So what are you saying?' he asked with a cynical twist to his features. 'That if you had known who I was you would not have fallen into my arms at all?'

How could she defend herself? Nikki wondered. Was there any way she could package what she had done to make it more palatable? At nineteen, she had been so very young and so heavily traumatised. She had wanted something different for herself, something so far removed from the dark, spreading stain of her childhood that she had accepted Joseph Ferliani's offer of a lucrative marriage contract without really looking into the details as closely as she should have. As the enormity of what she'd been committing herself to had begun to dawn, she had insisted on a few days to call her own before she signed away her future into his hands.

One last week of freedom.

And on the very first day of it Massimo Androletti had been the right man at the wrong time….

CHAPTER TWO

'CAN I buy you a drink?' Massimo said as she walked up to the bar the first night of her stay at the city hotel Joseph had paid for as part of their agreement.

Nikki turned her head and looked at the tall, dark, handsome man sitting with a glass of spirits half finished in front of him. He was dressed in a suit, but not just any old off-the-rack suit, one that fitted him superbly. She could tell he was taller than average by the way she had to raise her head to meet his brown, almost-black eyes as he got to his feet. She was five-foot-nine without heels, so it was a bit of a novelty to have to crane her neck for a change.

He had a thick head of curly dark hair but it was cut close to his scalp, as if he was a person who liked control. His jaw and chin were determined, if not a little forceful, and yet his smile was easy and involved his dark eyes in a totally compelling way.

'Why not?' she suddenly found herself replying. What had she got to lose? After the harrowing afternoon she'd just been through visiting her younger brother, a drink with a perfect stranger who knew nothing of her past was just what she needed. Besides, what was that quote: 'Eat, drink and be merry for tomorrow we die'?

'What would you like to drink?' he asked, leading her to one of the plush chairs in a quiet corner.

Nikki vaguely registered the hint of an Italian accent in his slightly formal use of English. How incredibly ironic, she thought. 'Champagne,' she said, and because she was feeling uncharacteristically reckless added, 'But not the cheap stuff, it gives me a headache. I want the best there is.'

'Then the best you will have,' he said, and signalled for the bar tender.

A couple of glasses later, Nikki ended up agreeing to have dinner with him, enjoying his company in a way she hadn't expected. She had been on very few dates; she hadn't been all that comfortable in the company of men other than her brother. But Massimo was charming and polite, amusing and attentive, and she couldn't help lapping it up while it lasted. But whenever the subject drifted into the territory of her background she papered over the cracks of her conscience with the parcel of lies she had constructed ever since the day her mother had died and her brother's life had been changed for ever.

'I'm a personal assistant,' she said, which at least was true. 'I'm having a week off. I thought I'd do some shopping, have some beauty treatments—you know, pamper myself a bit, that sort of thing.'

'You do not need beauty treatments,' he said, running his dark gaze over her. 'You are the most naturally beautiful woman I have ever met.'

A flicker of uncertainty momentarily flashed across her features. 'Do you really think so?' she asked in a soft, breathless whisper.

He leaned forward to take one of her hands in his, the curl of his fingers around hers sending shooting sparks of heat to her most secret place. 'Of course I think so,' he said. 'I have never met a more beautiful or desirable woman in my life.'

Nikki pulled her hand out of his to reach for her champagne glass, her stomach still flip-flopping all over the place. 'I'm sure you've met plenty of women much more attractive than me,' she said, her mouth going down at the corners.

'On the contrary, I have met very few that compare with your translucent beauty,' he said. 'Your blonde hair is like a skein of silk. Your eyes are the most amazing grey-blue and you are tall, slender and graceful. You are any man's dream.'

She looked at him searchingly. 'You don't think I'm too tall?'

He gave her a reproving look. 'You are surely not going to apologise for being tall, are you? You are doing my neck a huge favour. I do not have to bend down to hear what you are saying.'

Nikki giggled, which in itself was a novelty. She couldn't remember the last time she had found anything or anyone amusing. 'You're the first man in ages that I've looked up to,' she said, still smiling. 'It's quite a change, I can tell you.'

'Is there a current man in your life?' he asked.

Nikki hesitated for a fraction of a second. How could she tell him she was engaged to be married to a man twenty-five years older than her? A man who was offering her a passport out of the shame that had haunted and hunted her for so long.

'No,' she said, rationalising that for a week at least there was no one. She was a free agent until the following Saturday, and after that she was off the market for who knew how long.

'I find that hard to believe,' he said. 'What is wrong with all the young men in Melbourne?'

She smiled at him again, and took another sip of her champagne. 'What about you?' she asked. 'Are you currently unattached?'

'Yes,' he said on a little jagged sigh. 'I was involved with a woman in Sicily a few months back, but it did not work out.'

'Have you recently arrived from Italy?' she asked.

'I have dual citizenship,' he said. 'I travel back and forth a lot on business.'

'What sort of business?'

'I am building up an international investment portfolio. My plan is to seek ailing companies to buy and then resell them for a profit,' he said. 'With proper management teams in place, a flagging business can be turned around within a year or two, or even a few months.'

'It sounds very interesting, but rather expensive and extremely risky,' she commented.

'It is,' he agreed. 'I have a meeting later this week to hopefully organise financial backing for a company takeover I have planned for years.'

'You sound very determined,' she said, reaching for her glass and taking a little sip.

'I am.' A frown brought his dark brows together as he reached for his glass. 'The company I want to take over was launched using money defrauded from my father. He was swindled by someone he trusted as a friend. I am on a mission to get every cent of it back.'

Nikki felt a faint shiver run up her spine at the determination in his tone. His expression had darkened, his eyes losing their playfulness, and instead they had begun to glitter with hatred. 'So you're after revenge?' she asked.

He nodded grimly. 'It is all I think about. I want to take

my father's enemy down, and I will do so, even if it takes me a lifetime to achieve it.'

'How will you take him down?' she asked, her heart beginning to thud with alarm. 'You're not going to do anything...er...underhand, are you?'

He smiled at her worried expression. 'Of course I am not going to do anything illegal. I am simply going to outwit him in business. It should not be too hard. The best tactic in any sort of successful campaign is to know your enemy. I know all his weak spots, and so it will be relatively simple to disarm him when the time is right.'

'He sounds like a truly horrible person,' Nikki said, suppressing a tiny shudder. 'Is that why you're here?'

'Yes and no,' he said, his expression clouding slightly. 'I have some meetings to attend...' He appeared to give himself a mental shake and exchanged his serious expression for a smile. 'But enough about my troubles,' he went on in a lighter tone. 'Tell me about your family.'

Nikki felt her stomach drop with all-too-familiar panic. 'M-my family?'

'Yes; have you any brothers or sisters?' he asked.

She concentrated on the bubbles in her glass rather than meet his gaze. 'I have a brother two years younger than me.'

'What about your parents? Are they still married?'

'Yes,' she said, reflecting wryly that it was more or less true. Her mother had still been married to her father on the day he had taken her life and ruined Jayden's for ever.

'You are lucky to have come from such a loving and stable background,' Massimo said as he refilled the glasses. 'My parents divorced when I was sixteen.'

Lucky? Nikki almost laughed out loud. The last word she

would ever use to describe her background was 'lucky'. Each day had been a fight for survival, each night an agonising wait for disaster to unfold as soon as her father had walked through the door.

'Losing the business was bad enough, but losing my mother tipped him over.' He paused, as if searching for the words to continue, the flash of pain in his dark eyes all the more evident.

'What happened?' Nikki prompted gently.

His gaze meshed with hers. 'He took his life a few months later,' he said. 'I came out to the garage and found him unconscious. He had killed himself—the fumes had poisoned him, and he was unable to be revived.'

Nikki felt tears burn in her eyes for what he must have suffered. 'I am so sorry,' she said, reaching for his hand, her fingers curling around his. 'No wonder you are after revenge. This ghastly man took everything away from you.'

Massimo gave her another grim look. 'But I am going to get it all back, every single cent of it. I do not have the money to do it yet, but I will do it eventually. I know I will.'

'Do you know something, Massimo?' she said with an encouraging smile. 'I believe you will, too.'

He squeezed her hand. 'I have never met anyone like you before,' he said, his dark eyes melting as they held hers. 'I feel this amazing connection with you. Our backgrounds are very different, but I feel as if I have known you for a very long time—and yet we have only just met.'

Nikki felt her belly start to quiver as his long fingers stroked the underside of her wrist, the slow, sensual movement stirring her body into a whirlpool of feeling. Her breasts tightened, her nipples pressing against the lace of her bra as she held his dark-as-night gaze. 'I feel it too,' she said, her voice coming out low and husky.

A shadow of regret passed over his features. 'I am only here for a week,' he said. 'I have to go back to Italy first thing on Sunday. But, when I return, can I see you again?'

Nikki hoped he couldn't see the panic in her eyes as they came back to his. 'I'm sure you will have forgotten all about me by the time you return,' she said with a weak smile.

'No, Nikki,' he said, his fingers strong and determined around hers. 'I will *not* forget you.'

She moistened her lips with her tongue. 'I—I should have told you earlier,' she said, dropping her gaze as she hastily composed her lie. 'I don't come from Melbourne. I'm just here on a little holiday. I won't be here when you get back.'

'Where will you be?'

'Umm…Cairns.' She said the first place that came to mind.

'Then I will come and see you in Cairns,' he said. 'We can go to the Great Barrier Reef together, eh?'

'Massimo…' She forced her eyes to meet his. 'I'm not sure I'm the person you—'

'Do you believe in love at first sight?' he asked before she could finish her sentence.

A few hours ago Nikki would have answered a resounding 'no', but after spending the evening in Massimo's company she was now not so sure. She was attracted to him in a way she had never been attracted to anyone before, but it wasn't just a physical thing—although that in itself was as overwhelming as it could ever be. It was more a sense of being in the company of a man who stood up for what he believed in. His loyalty to his father's memory was truly admirable. It was so far removed from what she had experienced in her childhood she couldn't help but be impressed, and indeed incredibly moved.

She thought then what a wonderful husband and father he would make. His sense of family was so strong that no one would be hurt, while under his protection. He was quite simply the most amazing man she had ever met.

'You are taking a long time to answer.' Massimo sent her a rueful look. 'I have made a fool of myself, yes?'

'No,' she said, shivering all over again as he brought her hand up to his mouth. 'I'm not sure about love at first sight, but I definitely feel something I've never felt before.'

He pulled her to her feet, bringing her to stand in front of him. 'We have the next six days to explore and get to know each other,' he said. 'I do not want to rush you, but I cannot bear the thought of finding someone so special and wasting time in case we do not get this chance again.'

Nikki drew in a wobbly breath and did her best to smile. 'If it's meant to be, then we will get our chance,' she said as his mouth came down to hers.

CHAPTER THREE

NIKKI spent the happiest six days of her life in Massimo's company. She stalwartly refused to think about her wedding on Saturday. It was as if by not thinking about it she could really be the person Massimo believed her to be. She was a young carefree woman in love for the first time, relishing every moment of being truly adored and treated like a princess.

She knew it would have to end when the week was up, but she tried not to dwell on it too much. She comforted herself that Massimo was a man of the world. He would forget about her as soon as he boarded the plane back to Italy; his brief fling with the tall, blonde Australian girl would no doubt be a distant memory as soon as the first drink was served on the flight back home.

They explored the sights of Melbourne together, walking through the Bourke Street Mall to window shop, dining at some of the restaurants along the Southbank complex, and even spending some time at the world-famous Crown Casino where Nikki watched in awe as Massimo won a small fortune at one of the black-jack tables.

Later in the week they hired a car and visited the beautiful

Yarra Valley, notorious for its picturesque vineyards, where the rolling green hills and valleys they passed prompted Massimo to say how much it reminded him of Sicily.

'I would love to show you my homeland,' he said as they drove back after spending a wonderful afternoon at Healesville Wildlife Sanctuary. 'We do not have koalas and kangaroos and wombats, of course, but there are many wonderful historic buildings and artifacts.'

'I would love to travel the world one day,' Nikki said dreamily, looking out of the window as the verdant fields went by. 'I've only ever been to…' She stopped, her heart thumping at how close she had been to revealing how she had lied about where she had originally come from.

'You were saying?'

'Er…I've only ever lived in Australia,' she said. 'I know it's a big and diverse continent, but I haven't seen much of it really…'

He sent her a smile. 'You have no need to be ashamed, *cara*,' he said. 'You are young. You have plenty of time to see the world.'

On the last day Massimo arranged to meet her after he had his meeting in the city. As soon as she saw him walking towards her outside the art gallery, where she had spent the morning filling in time, she knew things had not gone well for him. His handsome face looked pinched and his mouth tight.

'Are you OK?' she asked, touching him on the arm.

He placed his hand over hers and gave it a tiny squeeze. 'I do not want to spoil our last afternoon and evening together talking about my business. Suffice to say things did not go according to plan.'

'I'm so sorry.'

He gave her a strained smile. 'I will just have to wait a little longer to achieve what I want, but then the best things in life are worth waiting for, no?'

'I guess…' she answered, looking down at their linked hands.

They walked past the Shrine of Remembrance through to the Botanic Gardens, stopping to have afternoon tea at the café overlooking the lake, where ducks waddled in search of crumbs and cheeky sparrows darted in amongst the chairs and tables in spite of the shooing actions of the staff.

Massimo smiled indulgently as she surreptitiously bent down to scatter some crumbs from the coconut cake he'd bought her. 'You are not supposed to encourage them,' he said, indicating the Do Not Feed the Birds sign nearby.

'I know, but I can't help feeling sorry for them,' she said, a fleeting shadow of sadness moving across her face. 'They've probably got little babies to feed.'

He reached across the table for her hand and brought it up to his mouth, kissing each fingertip in turn, his intense gaze holding hers. 'You have such a kind and tender heart,' he said in a deep, gravelly tone. 'I have waited a long time to meet someone as sensitive to the needs of others as you are.'

Nikki gently pulled her hand out of his, her whole body tingling with awareness. As each day had passed, she'd found it harder and harder to resist him. He had not pressured her to sleep with him, which surprised her. She had assumed, like many men with his jet-setting lifestyle, that he would have leaped at the chance of a one-week fling with a woman he had singled out for his attention. His kisses had been passionate and tender, enthralling and tantalising, and yet each time their mouths had touched he seemed to be keeping himself in check.

'You are feeling nervous and uncertain, *cara*?' he asked into the little silence.

'W-what do you mean?'

He reached for her hand again and began stroking the sensitive skin on the underside of her wrist in slow, sensual movements that sent a riot of sensation to her toes and back. 'I want you,' he stated bluntly. 'I have wanted you from the first moment I saw you but something about you made me realise you are not a one-night stand sort of girl. I deeply respect that about you.'

Somehow she found her voice in time to croak out, 'T-thank you.'

'I have a bit of a reputation for working hard and playing harder,' he confessed. 'I can assure you, it is highly unusual for me to have spent more than three dates with a woman before bedding her.'

Nikki swallowed.

He smiled at the twin flags of colour on her cheeks. 'You are a virgin, yes?'

Her eyes fell away from his. 'No,' she said in a small voice. 'I wish I still was. My first and only time was horrible…'

He frowned, and his hand encircling her wrist tightened protectively. 'You were…' he paused over the word '…raped?'

Her eyes came back to his, her colour still high. 'No, I just didn't realise it would be so…so one-sided, if you know what I mean.'

His fingers began their sensual magic against the satin surface of her skin. 'You did not experience pleasure, Nikki?'

'Not really.' She gave a little wry grimace and added, 'Not at all, actually.'

His eyes darkened with tenderness as he pulled her to her feet. 'We have one night left, *cara*,' he said, linking her arm through his. 'I want to make it as memorable as possible.'

Nikki had not dreamt how truly memorable it would be. They went back to the hotel hand in hand, the silence that hung between them heavy and pulsing with promise.

She felt it all through their last dinner together in the hotel restaurant. Each time his eyes caught and held hers, she sensed the sexual tension building in him. She could feel it thrumming in her own body, a deep and low pulse that begged to be assuaged.

She felt it in the lift as they silently climbed the floors to his room, each number showing above their heads like a countdown to paradise.

And she felt it in the thudding pulse in his fingers as they tilted her face to receive his kiss, the self-control he had been reining in all week finally slipping as the door of his room closed behind them.

'I should not be doing this,' he said, pressing hot kisses to the side of her neck as he lifted her hair out of the way. 'I told myself I would wait until I return from Sicily, but I want you so much I am burning inside and out with it.'

Nikki raised her face for more of his drugging kisses. 'I want you too,' she whispered against his lips. 'I want you to make love to me. I want to feel pleasure... Your pleasure as well as mine.'

He held her from him, looking deeply into her eyes. 'Are you absolutely sure, *cara*? I can wait for you. I will *make* myself wait for you if you do not feel ready to take this step.'

She pulled his mouth back down to hers. 'Don't make

me wait,' she pleaded desperately. 'I don't want to wait another minute.'

He undressed her, the slow movements of his hands belying the true state of his arousal. She felt it against her, the hard surge of his body and how he fought to control it in order to prepare her properly for his passionate possession. His mouth was on hers, and then on each of her breasts, sucking gently at first, and then harder until her back arched with intense longing.

He laid her carefully on the king-sized bed, trailing a hot blaze of kisses all over her body, her mouth, her neck, her breasts and the tiny cave of her belly button before moving lower. She totally melted under the sweep and stroke of his tongue as it separated her feminine folds, the sensation of such an intimate caress sending her pulse skyrocketing. Her body began to convulse, the earth-shattering release beyond anything she had ever imagined.

He waited until she was calm once more before reaching for a condom. She watched with wide eyes as he came back to her, taking his time again in kissing and caressing her, until she was begging him to fill her. 'Oh, please…oh please…'

'You are getting impatient, Nikki,' he said playfully, kissing her lingeringly, the sexy saltiness of her own body on his lips inciting her to grab at him greedily, her pelvis rising to meet the downward thrust of his.

Nikki heard his deep groan of pleasure as the small, tight sheath of her body grasped at him, the honeyed warmth enveloping him totally. He tried to control his thrusts to keep them slow and not too deep, but she was having none of it. She clung to him, her fingers digging into the tautness of his buttocks to keep him where she wanted him.

She felt herself begin to climb the mountain again, the pinnacle getting closer and closer with each surging movement of his body within hers.

The overwhelming power of his release surprised her, as did her own. It was like an earthquake rumbling between them, rocking them back and forth, shaking them, shattering them into a thousand tiny pieces.

She held him against her as his breathing gradually came back to normal, the skin of his back raised in tiny goose-bumps, under the soft pads of her fingertips.

He lifted himself up on his elbows to look at her, his dark eyes full of wonder. 'Do you realise what you have just done, Nikki?' he asked.

'W-what?' she asked, a shadow of uncertainty flitting across her face.

'You have made me fall in love with you,' he said. 'For ever.'

Nikki felt her throat tighten. Oh God! What had she done? This should not have happened. She should *not* have let it happen. She had no right to sleep with a man to whom she could offer nothing but a one-night stand, for that was all it could ever be.

He reached past her to take something out of the bedside drawer. 'I have something for you,' he said.

Nikki tensed as he retrieved the small package. Throughout the week he had bought her gifts—not expensive ones, which had made it easy for her to accept them, with perhaps not an entirely clear conscience, but she'd reasoned she wanted something to keep as a reminder of what she could have had if life had dealt her a different hand of cards.

She took the tiny package from him, her fingers beginning to tremble slightly as she felt the cushioning of velvet beneath the tissue wrapping. 'What is it?' she asked, her voice sounding rusty.

'Open it and see,' he said, smiling at her.

She began to undo the tiny silk ribbon, each movement of her fingers meticulously slow. The tissue fell away, and the red velvet box lay in her hand like a square of blood. She knew what was in it before she opened it, knew too that she should have handed it straight back and told him the truth, but instead she slowly lifted the lid.

A diamond solitaire ring gleamed up at her, its sheer brilliance taking her breath away.

'Put it on,' he said into the silence.

Nikki had never hated herself more than at that moment. The shame of her past was nothing to what she was experiencing now. But as if her fingers had a mind of their own they lifted the ring from its velvet home, and slid it on her ring finger where Joseph Ferliani's ring was supposed to be. But, unlike the heavy, cumbersome cluster Joseph had insisted she wear, Massimo's ring was exquisitely delicate, suiting her slim hand perfectly.

'Will you marry me, Nikki?' Massimo asked as he took her hand in his. 'I know this is terribly rushed, but I love you and want to spend the rest of my life with you.'

Nikki bit her lip in anguish, tears springing in a crystal stream from her eyes as she met his. 'I don't know what to say…' she began. 'It's been so sudden…so totally unexpected.'

He brought her closer to the warmth of his body and, holding her hand to his heart, smiled down at her. 'It looks like I will have to be patient and wait for your answer on my return,' he said. 'That will give you time to talk it over with your family. I am forgetting how very young you are. I am nine years older than you, so it is reasonable to expect you to be feeling a bit overwhelmed—especially now, after we have made love for the very first time.'

She *was* overwhelmed, but with guilt. It prodded and poked at her from every angle like a thousand pointed daggers. How could she have let things get to this stage? What had she been thinking? She should have known from the beginning that a man like Massimo Androletti would want more than a quick fling. She should have had one drink with him that first night and left, then he would not have had to suffer the pain of rejection, and she would not have known what it felt like to be truly in love, only to have to walk away because of circumstances beyond her control.

'Massimo, there's something I need to tell you…'

He bent his head to press a soft kiss to her mouth. 'No, *cara*,' he said. 'Do not give me your answer until we meet again. I am flying to Palermo on Sunday. I am sorry I cannot spend the day with you tomorrow, but I have an engagement to attend which I cannot get out of.'

'It's all right,' she said, inwardly blowing out a breath of relief. 'I have something on as well.'

He held her close, his arms strong and protective around her. 'I will miss you, Nikki. Every day we are apart I will miss you.'

'Me too,' she whispered, her heart breaking into a million pieces.

He put her from him. 'I will not say goodbye, but *vederla presto*.'

She looked up at him in puzzlement. 'What does that mean?'

'It means "see you soon",' he said, and sealed his promise with a burning kiss.

CHAPTER FOUR

NIKKI arrived at the church in her stiff-as-meringue dress, the lace itching her all over as she walked up the aisle, her bouquet feeling as heavy as her heart in her hands. She didn't recognise any of the faces, but then it wasn't as if she had a large circle of friends to invite. Ever since she'd moved from Perth with Jayden, there hadn't been time to socialise even if she had felt inclined to do so. Holding down a job in order to pay for her brother's care had taken up every bit of available time.

She just wanted this bit to be over so she could help her younger brother get the extra support he needed. Joseph had offered her a large sum of money in exchange for her hand in marriage. He had told her he needed a trophy wife, and was prepared to pay her a wage on top of the amount he'd promised for as long as she lived with him. He had assured her he was not interested in consummating the union due to his health problems, which he'd insisted no one was to know about. To all intents and purposes, their marriage was to appear normal, and Nikki had only agreed because she knew it would be worth it to see Jayden settled into Rosedale House where he would receive the twenty-four-hour care he so desperately needed.

Finally the vows were over, the register signed and the organ playing as they came out of the church to a cloud of confetti.

It was only then that Nikki saw him.

She stumbled in her tracks, her hand digging into Joseph's arm to steady herself as Massimo Androletti stepped from the crowd to stand in front of them, his black gaze glittering with a rage so intense she felt as if her skin was going to peel away layer by sensitive layer under its scorching heat.

'I would like to be introduced to your new wife,' he said, addressing Joseph in a seemingly polite tone, although the way he said the word 'wife' made it sound more like an insult.

'Nikki,' Joseph said, 'this is my stepson, Massimo Androletti, who has graced us with his presence this afternoon, after telling me for weeks he wouldn't be seen dead at any wedding of mine. Massimo, this is Nikki, my new wife.'

'Il piacere è tutto mio,' Massimo said, and with a sardonic curl of his lip translated, 'The pleasure is all mine.'

Nikki felt the heat of his fingers as he took her hand, the hint of steel in them as they brought it up to his mouth sending a tremor of terror through her body. She knew her face was every shade of red, but there was nothing she could do about it. She had never dreamed that such a fateful coincidence could occur, but, thinking back over the last week, she realised there had been a hundred clues if she had taken the time to reflect on them. But then she hadn't wanted to think about anything, but that precious time with Massimo, for she'd known it had to end.

'So you decided to come after all,' Joseph said to Massimo. 'What changed your mind?'

'I had heard you were marrying your new secretary,' Massimo said, swinging his hardened gaze to Nikki, running it up and down her body insultingly. 'But I had no idea she was so very young and beautiful.'

Joseph's arm came around Nikki's waist in a territorial manner. 'She is to be the new face of the Ferliani Fashions advertising campaign. She is delightful, is she not?'

'Exquisite,' Massimo drawled insolently. 'But then you always want the best, and do whatever you can to get it.'

Joseph gave him an imperious smile. 'Get over it, Massimo. This is one time you are not going to win. I have it all—a beautiful wife, a business that is thriving, and money to play with.'

'What a pity none of it is really yours,' Massimo ground out, his eyes flashing. 'Even your angelic-looking wife is a slut. Why don't you ask her what she was doing all last week?'

Nikki felt the colour of her shame brand her from head to foot. She wanted to sink to the ground at their feet, but a last vestige of pride made her hold her head high.

'Nikki was having a well-earned rest before the wedding,' Joseph said, but even she could see the doubt in his hazel eyes as they came to rest on her. 'Weren't you, Nikki?'

'T-that's right,' she answered, lowering her gaze slightly.

'Yes, well, she certainly spent a lot of time relaxing,' Massimo said with another venomous glance in her direction. 'But perhaps you had better ask her whose bed she was in last night.'

'I think it might be time for you to leave,' Joseph said, indicating for one of his burly staff members to come forward. 'Gino, please show Signore Androletti the way out.'

'You lying little whore,' Massimo said to Nikki as he brushed off the man's hands as if they were pieces of lint. 'I will make you pay for this. I will not rest until I have you begging for my mercy, I swear to God.'

Nikki swallowed convulsively as he stalked out of the church grounds, the tolling of the bells ringing in her ears like an omen for the future…

The car coming to a halt jolted Nikki out of the past. She felt Massimo's burning gaze still pressing against her in accusation. 'You knew who I was that first night, didn't you, Nikki? It was all a game to you, to make me appear a lovesick fool, while you were busily planning your marriage to another man—the one man I hated more than any other.'

'You are entitled to your opinion, but I can assure you it is wrong. Anyway, it was a long time ago,' she said with carefully measured calm. 'It can hardly have any relevance to here and now.'

'It has *everything* to do with here and now,' he returned with chilling determination. 'You see, Nikki, the time has come for my revenge.'

Nikki refused to allow him the satisfaction of seeing how much his words frightened her. She sat casually in her seat, one finely arched brow lifting in scorn. 'This is the twenty-first century, in case you hadn't noticed. The days of an eye for an eye, and what have you, have long gone.'

'We will see,' he said, and unfolded himself from the car. He turned to offer her a hand, but she ignored it as she too exited the vehicle on legs that were not as steady as she would have liked.

She looked up at the imposing mansion before throwing him a questioning glance. 'I take it this is your house?' she said.

'It is.' He turned to the driver. 'Ricardo, you can take the next couple of hours off. Mrs Ferliani and I have business to discuss. I will call you when I need you.'

'Right, boss.'

Nikki pulled her mouth tight as the limousine drove away. 'I have no desire to discuss anything with you,' she said. 'I have things to see to at home, in any case.'

His dark brows lifted expressively. 'Home?' he asked. 'Now, which home are you referring to, I wonder?'

She ground her teeth. 'Even if what you say is true, that the house is now yours, by law I don't have to move out without notice.'

'On the contrary, as the new owner I can evict you at a moment's notice,' he said. 'You have already been living there for several months rent-free—or did your husband not inform you of that?'

Nikki swallowed against the solid lump of dread in her throat. 'What are you talking about?' she asked, her heart stumbling in her chest.

He gave her a cool smile. 'Your husband approached me for financial help in the months before he died. He begged me to dig him out of trouble—but of course I refused.'

'You unfeeling bastard,' she bit out. 'How could you twist the knife like that in a dying man?'

'As you know, I had a score to settle,' he said. 'He took it very well, all things considered. He handed me everything—the house, the cars, the business, and...' He paused deliberately, his gaze locking meaningfully with hers.

Don't ask, Nikki told herself firmly. *You already know the answer, so what would be the point?*

'You do not want to know what else your husband put up for purchase?' he asked.

She met his sardonic gaze with a flare of resentment in hers.

'If by any chance you are presuming to lump *me* in with the goods and chattels, then forget it—I am *not* for sale.'

His smile didn't quite reach his eyes as he came to stand right in front of her. 'He paid you to marry him,' he said. 'He even told me how much. You put quite a high price on yourself, did you not?'

Nikki ran her tongue over her dry lips as his eyes burned into hers. She refused to answer out of a mixture of pride and anger. Let him think what he liked. What did it matter now? Joseph was dead, and if what Massimo had said was true she was going to have to find a way to scrape what she could together to keep Jayden in care. She'd been down on her luck before and pulled herself out of it. It would be hard, but she'd damn well do it for her brother's sake.

'Of course, I will be very generous in my payment for your services,' he said. 'Very generous, indeed.'

She clenched her fists at her sides, her chest heaving against the tide of anger raging within her. 'I am *not* going to sleep with you,' she said. 'Not for any price.'

The look he gave her was full of icy disdain. 'You are very convincing, but I know what you are up to, Nikki. You are used to a high standard of living. You want to make sure it continues, do you not?'

Nikki felt as if her heart was being crushed between two solid bookends. 'Joseph would not have left me with nothing,' she said again, dearly hoping it was true. 'He told me I would be left well-provided for on his death.'

'I already told you, Nikki. Were you not listening? He left you with nothing. Nothing but debts that will take you years to clear, but fortunately for you I have come up with a plan to help you offload them more or less immediately.'

Nikki moistened her lips again, panic beating like a primitive tribal drum inside her chest. 'What p-plan would that be?' she asked, wishing her voice didn't sound so thin and scared.

He gave her one of his inscrutable looks. 'I want you to be my mistress of convenience.'

She frowned as she tried to make sense of his statement. 'I'm afraid you'll have to explain what you mean,' she said after a heart-chugging pause. 'I'm unfamiliar with the term.'

'I have recently ended a relationship,' he informed her in a dispassionate tone. 'The woman I was involved with is not finding it easy to let go. I have always found the best way to deal with such stubbornness is to have physical evidence that I have now moved on with my life.'

'I'm still not sure what it is you want me to do,' she said guardedly.

'You are being deliberately obtuse, are you not?' he asked. 'I want you to do everything for me that you did for my stepfather.'

Nikki couldn't imagine Joseph revealing the unconsummated nature of their relationship, and wondered if he had told Massimo a mountain of lies instead in an effort to maintain his sense of male pride.

Massimo waved a hand towards the mansion behind him. 'You see this house?' he asked.

She looked past his shoulder at the huge, two-storey mock-Georgian building before bringing her gaze back to his. 'Yes…'

'I want you to move in with me.'

Her eyes widened. 'I'm afraid that's out of the question,' she said. 'I can't possibly live with you.'

He gave her an ironic glance. 'You find the position I am offering beneath you?'

She narrowed her eyes at him. 'What's this about, Massimo? Some petty payback scheme to make me regret our stupid little fling five years ago?'

'I need a trophy mistress,' he said. 'You need a job—it is as simple as that.'

Nikki felt her stomach lurch sideways in alarm. 'I already have a job, if you remember,' she said, moistening her bone-dry lips again. 'I am still the face of Ferliani Fashions. I only took off the last six months to nurse Joseph.'

His eyes were unreadable as they held hers. 'As the new owner and CEO of Ferliani Fashions, I have decided not to renew your contract,' he said. 'I have other plans for you.'

She gave him a fiery glare. 'What do you want me to do, scrub your floors and fold your socks?'

'That, and a whole lot more.'

Her eyes narrowed into wary slits. 'How much more?'

'I have a busy life,' he said. 'I do not have time to cook proper meals or maintain an immaculate house. Joseph told me what a wonderful wife you were in that respect. He told me how you refused to have a housekeeper—that you preferred to do it yourself. I need someone running things here twenty-four-seven. I am willing to pay you generously for each month the arrangement continues.' He named a sum that sent her brows winging upwards, and added, 'It is twice what you were earning from the Ferliani contract.'

'There are hundreds of women who would give anything to have this job,' she said. 'But I'm not interested.'

'Ah, but you have no choice, Nikki,' he said. 'For if you do not agree you will have to pay back every cent of the money your husband borrowed from me in your name a month before he died. Your signature is on the documents.'

Nikki stared at him, cold fear trickling into every one of her veins like a flow of ice. She vaguely remembered Joseph pushing some papers under her nose, mumbling something about advertising expenses. It had been an astonishing amount of money, she recalled with another quake of apprehension. But she had signed her name and felt grateful that he was taking care of the business side of things while he still could, never realising it would lead to this.

'You've been planning this for months, haven't you?' she bit out caustically. 'You've been watching and waiting like a vulture circling overhead for your stepfather to die.'

'I told you five years ago when we met that I would have my revenge on what he did. He stole my father's money and launched the Ferliani label using it,' he said. 'But I must say my motivation increased even more after our brief assignation. There's a certain irony in it, don't you think? We have come full circle. You are the face of Ferliani Fashions only because my stepfather gave you the leg up you needed, but I now own the company. You do not have a future without me. You need me, Nikki, whether you like it or not. You need me.'

Her grey-blue eyes glittered with sparks of fury. 'You're asking for my degradation, that's what you're doing.'

He gave her a cool, composed smile in return. 'I am not *asking* anything of you, Nikki. I am *telling* you what is going to happen.'

'And I am telling you to go to hell!' she said and, spinning on her heels, began to stalk down the long crushed-lime-stone driveway.

'If you take even one step outside that gate, I will activate legal proceedings immediately to recoup the money you owe me—every last cent of it,' Massimo said in an indomitable tone.

Nikki's right foot hovered over the boundary line as she thought about her choices. There was so much she didn't know. Joseph's business affairs had always seemed to her to be a little on the complicated side. He'd had money coming in from various local and international investors to float the label, and, while she had been quite content to leave him to it, so she could do her part in fulfilling the modelling contract, she'd known it was quite possible debts had mounted up over the months before he'd finally succumbed to the cancer that he'd been valiantly fighting ever since she'd met him.

The modelling meant nothing to her; it had always been a means to an end. She had hidden behind it, enjoying the benefits of financial security in order to rise above her impoverished background. No one knew that the glamorous Nikki Ferliani was actually Nicola Jenkins, the eldest child of Kaylene and Frank Jenkins, brought up surrounded by poverty, violence and crime. And certainly no one knew her father was serving a life sentence for murder, with 'never to be released' stamped on his file.

Not even Joseph had known about that.

And then there was Jayden.

He was happy at Rosedale House, or at least as happy as someone with permanent and severe physical and mental disabilities could be. The level of care he received there was the best that money could buy. If she had to move him away from the dedicated staff who had grown so fond of him, she would never be able to forgive herself. After all, wasn't it her fault he had been injured in the first place?

She slowly turned around, her expression stripped of all

emotion as she faced her nemesis. 'I need some time to think about this.'

'You have the next ten seconds,' he said, lifting his wrist to look at his watch, and began to count them. 'Nine, eight, seven six, five—'

'All right,' she said, her stomach somersaulting in dread at what was ahead. 'I will be your…er…trophy mistress.'

His eyes came back to hers, his inbuilt cynicism glinting in their smoky depths. 'I knew you would see sense. You are far too mercenary to throw away a fortune such as this.'

She ran her tongue over the desert dryness of her lips. 'When do you want me to…to start?'

He reached into the pocket of his trousers and brought out a set of keys. He walked to where she was standing, took her clenched fist and, unpeeling her stiff fingers, placed the keys in her palm. 'You started five minutes ago,' he said.

Nikki closed her fingers around the cold metal of the keys, wincing as they bit into the soft flesh of her palm.

Now, there's another irony, she thought as she followed him a moment later into the Toorak mansion. Within her very own hand lay the keys to her new prison…

CHAPTER FIVE

IT WAS a stunningly beautiful house. It was decorated throughout in subtle tones of cream and taupe and white, offset superbly by the black wrought-iron of the balustrade on the magnificent staircase leading to the upper floor. The marbled floor of the elegant foyer led into ankle-deep caramel-brown carpet in the living areas, the large windows offering wonderful views of the lush and very private gardens outside.

It was a house built for entertaining and pleasure, every room ideally appointed for large numbers with maximum comfort.

The furniture as well as the artworks on the walls spoke of unlimited wealth and dignified taste. It was nothing like the ostentatious layout Joseph had insisted on in his house in South Yarra, and certainly nothing like the variety of rundown trailer parks where Nikki had spent most of her childhood.

'I have taken the liberty of organising someone to collect your belongings from your previous residence.' Massimo's deep voice broke the silence. 'They will be delivered here tomorrow. All you will need to do is pack your personal things. They will do the rest.'

Nikki turned to look at him. 'Aren't you rushing things a bit?' she asked. 'I have been a widow only a week, now I am supposedly your mistress. What will people think?'

He gave an indifferent shrug. 'I do not care for what people think. This is between you and me. The press will no doubt begin to speculate, which brings me to the issue of what we will tell other people.'

'How about the truth?' she said with an arch look. 'That you are blackmailing me for revenge.'

His dark eyes glinted warningly as they held hers. 'It would be in your interests to refrain from revealing the real motivations behind our relationship—both your own and mine.'

'I'm not going to pretend to be in love with you,' she said with a resentful scowl.

He gave her a cynical smile. 'That would indeed be a rather tall order, eh, Nikki? Although you did it quite convincingly in the past, I seem to recall.'

'You're never going to let it go, are you?' she asked with a flash of ire in her grey-blue eyes. 'Your stupid male pride got dented, and now five years later you're still harping on about it.'

He came up close and took her chin between his finger and thumb, his eyes blazing with hatred as he ground out savagely, 'I told you the day you married my stepfather that one day I would have you begging for my mercy. Do not tempt me to make it *this* day, the very day you buried him.'

Nikki swallowed back her fear, her heart chugging like an old engine going uphill. 'L-let me go,' she croaked.

His fingers tightened momentarily, the fire of his gaze raking her face for endless seconds, before he dropped his hand and stepped back from her.

Nikki felt her breath leave her chest in a ragged whoosh, her chin still tingling where his fingers had lain. She wanted to reach up and touch her skin, but knew it would give away her vulnerability, so she clenched her hands into hard little fists by her sides.

'I will send a car for you at 10 a.m. tomorrow,' he said. 'The house you have been living in is going to be redecorated and sold.'

'Removing every last trace of him, are you?' she sniped at him bitterly. 'Isn't that a bit melodramatic even for someone as stuck in the Middle Ages as you?'

Twin spots of white-tipped anger were visible at both sides of his tightened mouth. 'You will have to learn to curb that tongue of yours, Nikki. You might have wound my stepfather around your little finger, but you will not achieve the same success with me. I expect you to be polite and charming at all times, most particularly when we are entertaining guests. I have important clients, corporate investors, who will expect you to be the perfect hostess.'

'So you're expecting me to cook for you, are you?'

'My stepfather informed me of your many talents, both in and out of the kitchen,' he said with another searing look over her heaving form. 'I am sure you will be able to handle the challenge of rustling up a few ingredients from time to time.'

'I'm surprised you haven't made me audition for the part,' she said. 'How do you know Joseph wasn't lying about my capabilities?'

His eyes were steady on hers. 'My stepfather was an inveterate liar and a cheat, but the one thing he had no reason to lie about was his relationship with you. He made no secret of how you gave him pleasure, catering to his every physical need in spite of the difference in your age.'

Nikki felt ill at what he was implying. Surely Joseph hadn't taken things to that extreme in a last-ditch attempt to maintain his male pride?

'I will leave you for a few minutes to wander around the house, to get acquainted with its layout.' Massimo filled the silence. 'You can choose any room you like, but it might be preferable to keep it well away from mine.'

'Why?' she asked with a deliberately taunting look. 'Are you worried you might be tempted to go back on your promise?'

His gaze ran over her indolently. 'No,' he said. 'I am not. For, if you recall, I did not promise anything of that nature.'

Nikki felt her face suffuse with red-hot heat as the significance of his statement began to sink in. 'You're surely not expecting me to sleep with you, are you? You said I was to be a trophy mistress.'

His expression was difficult to read. 'And that is what you will be, unless one or both of us changes our mind.'

She turned away, pretending an avid interest in the view from the window overlooking the garden, her head pounding with uncertainty and fear.

He had control of everything.

How could she have not anticipated this? She had seen the hatred in his look five years ago but had foolishly deluded herself into thinking he would get over it.

He had not done so.

'You…you have a lovely garden,' she said, for the want of something to fill the uncomfortable silence.

'You are at liberty to enjoy it at your leisure,' he said. 'I do not expect you to slave your fingers to the bone.'

She turned back to face him, cynicism sharpening her features. 'So I won't be chained to the house?' she asked.

'Not at all. You can come and go as you please, but there are some ground rules.'

She folded her arms across her chest. 'Which are?'

'No men.'

She twisted her mouth at him. 'Please allow me some measure of decency. In case you have forgotten, I have just buried my husband.'

'Good, for I will not tolerate you entertaining any of your lovers in my house.'

She straightened her spine and glared at him. 'Anything else?' she asked.

'Yes,' he said. 'I expect you to be polite at all times to the young woman who will be replacing you as the face of Ferliani Fashions—Abriana Cavello. She may on occasion come to the house. I will try to keep such visits to a minimum, but if she should be here, I will expect you to treat her just like any other guest.'

Nikki felt her anger towards him skyrocket. She knew how this was going to work; she could feel it in her bones. No doubt this Cavello woman had slept with him to gain his favour and was now going to flounce around the house, acting like a prima donna just to needle her into breaking one of his stupid rules.

'That shouldn't be a problem,' she said, grinding her teeth. 'I am sure we will get along just fine.'

'That will be all for now,' he said, turning away to leaf through some papers he'd picked up from the hall table. 'I will be in my study when you have finished looking over the house.'

'And then?'

He put the papers to one side and met her arched-brow look. 'And then, Nikki, we will have dinner together.'

'Dinner?'

He smiled wryly at her anxious expression. 'Do not worry. I do not expect you to cook tonight. We will go out this evening.'

'Thank you for being so considerate,' she said with heavy sarcasm. 'But if it's all the same to you, I would prefer to go straight home.'

His black-diamond stare clashed with hers. 'You no longer *have* a home, and if I say we will have dinner together then that is what we will do, do you understand?'

Nikki felt like she was standing in front of a stranger. Gone was the gentle and loving Massimo Androletti of five years ago, and in his place was a hard, cold, determined man intent on exacting every gram of revenge he could.

She hated having to bow to his command, but there was nothing else she could do short of telling him about her reasons for marrying his stepfather. But it wasn't just her pride that wouldn't allow her to do it. If she told him who she really was—the daughter of a man who had committed the most heinous of crimes—how could she be sure it wouldn't be all over the papers within hours? Massimo was after revenge, and what better revenge could he have than to bring her past to light?

She drew in a breath, the air feeling like acid as it expanded her lungs. 'It seems I have no say in the matter. You are now the boss.'

'In every sense of the word,' he said. 'You will answer to no one but me until such time that I feel your debt is cleared.'

'How long are you planning this façade of a relationship to last?' she asked.

'It will last as long as I say. Considering what happened between us the last time, I think you owe me that privilege, don't you?'

'In my opinion, I don't owe you a thing,' she said. 'Or I wouldn't if you hadn't exploited Joseph's illness the way you did.'

'Do not speak to me of that man,' he bit out furiously. 'Once we are living together tomorrow you are forbidden to mention his name in my company. Do you understand?'

Nikki held his glittering glare with wavering courage. 'You might be able to stop me saying his name, but you can't stop me from thinking about him,' she said.

Her words angered him more than she had anticipated. She saw the flash of fury come and go in his eyes as they clashed with hers, and her stomach gave a little shudder of trepidation. She had underestimated him all those years ago. She had thought his generous and loving nature would recover quickly from her rejection, but instead it had created something she wasn't sure she could handle.

He came back to stand in front of her, his hand beneath her chin this time like a burning brand. 'Then I will have to find a way to make you stop thinking about him, won't I, Nikki?'

Her eyes went to his mouth, the hard, embittered line of it sending her stomach into another nosedive of panic. If he should kiss her, he would know how terribly vulnerable she was towards him. He would assume she was exchanging one rich man for another, never once realising she had only ever loved him.

His thumb traced a sensuous pathway across the cushioned bow of her bottom lip, back and forth, in a careless movement that stirred her longing for him like a long-handled spoon in her belly. She held her breath, mentally preparing herself for the descent of his mouth, when he stepped away from her without warning.

'I will be in my study if you should need me,' he said. 'I will have Ricardo pick us up in half an hour.'

She watched him leave the room, disappointment deflating her chest along with the almost inaudible sound of her rough-edged sigh.

After she'd given the house a quick once-over, Nikki chose the smallest bedroom five doors down from what she presumed to be Massimo's. She had poked her head in, seen the huge bed and *en suite* leading off it, and had quickly surmised it was his domain. She could even smell him in the air, the clean male scent combined with his signature aftershave, the citrus and sandalwood aftershave she had still been able to smell on her skin the day she had married Joseph Ferliani.

She shut the door firmly and moved on, determined to separate herself from the tempting lure of the past. She didn't want to think about how it had felt that one precious time to have her body pinned beneath the hard, surging pressure of Massimo's. She didn't want to be reminded of how he had trailed hot kisses down her body, from her peaking breasts to her quivering thighs, his lips and tongue wreaking havoc on all of her senses. She didn't want to remember the arch of her spine as his body had taken her to paradise, the aftershocks of pleasure triggering his own release as he'd spilled himself into her silky warmth.

She didn't want to remember how she had sobbed in the loneliness of her bed for months after her marriage to Joseph, her heart breaking for what she had lost.

Massimo stared sightlessly at the documents in front of him. They represented everything he had worked so hard for, but somehow he felt as if something was missing. It was an empty victory when the one prize he had longed for had already been snapped up by someone else. He had seen the sadness in Nikki's grey-blue eyes as his stepfather's coffin had been lowered into the ground.

He hadn't been expecting that.

He had her marked as a gold-digger; why else had she married Joseph Ferliani after spending such a phenomenally sensuous night with *him* all those years ago? Quite obviously she had cold-heartedly calculated the bigger returns. He had told her repeatedly over that week that he was still building his business. She had done the sums and come up with Joseph as the one to back with her body and her misleadingly sultry smile.

He clenched his fists where they lay on the desk. She would pay for it. She would pay for it every moment she spent in his house.

Of that he would make sure.

Nikki sat silently beside Massimo as his driver took them to the city, her heart beginning to thud a little unevenly when she realised where they were heading. She stiffened in her seat when the hotel where they had spent that glorious week together came into view. She hadn't been able to bring herself back in all the time she had been married to Joseph. She had come close once or twice, but had never been able to put herself through it, knowing that as soon as she walked in those doors, her longing for what might have been would overwhelm her all over again.

She clutched her bag to her chest as the car came to a halt. 'I'm not getting out,' she said.

'You have the choice of getting out of the car under your own volition, or being subjected to me carrying you into the hotel restaurant,' Massimo informed her in a tone that was undergirded by steel. 'Which is it to be?'

Nikki threw him a blistering glare. 'You're doing this deliberately, aren't you? All of this is part of your stupid revenge-plot.'

'For tonight we are two people having dinner together,' he returned. 'There is no other agenda.'

'With you there is always an agenda,' she said, scowling at him furiously. 'There are thousands of restaurants in Melbourne—why did it have to be this one?'

'It is a nice restaurant, and the view over the city is superb.'

'You brought me here to rub salt in the wound,' she said. 'You knew it would upset me.'

'I do not see why it should upset you, Nikki,' he said. 'After all, it is not as if *I* married someone else the day after we last dined here. That was you—remember?'

Nikki wasn't sure it would be wise to answer. She had already given too much away as it was. She should have feigned indifference, played it cool and composed, instead of emotionally fragile.

The trouble was it wasn't possible for her to be cool and

composed around Massimo, not while she still harboured feelings for him. Her love for him had never gone away; she'd wondered many times over the last five years if it ever would. Even in the face of his hatred she still felt the steady, strong pulse of her love for him beating inside her.

The uniformed man held the door open for her, and, taking a shaky breath, she exited the car, and with Massimo's hand at her elbow she reluctantly allowed herself to be led inside.

The hotel had undergone considerable refurbishment in the time since they'd last been there, but Nikki still felt the press of memories coming towards her from every corner of the foyer and lounge-bar area.

She had sat in that quiet area near the windows, listening intently to Massimo's plans for the future, had smiled at his jokes, held his hand, shared his cocktails and dreamed of a magical life where she could have it all.

'I thought before dinner we would have a drink in the bar for old times' sake.' His voice intruded on her reverie.

Nikki knew it would be pointless refusing, so forced her legs to carry her to the plush sofas a short distance from the white grand-piano. She sat down and looked at the drinks menu, hardly able to read a word for the sudden blur of tears.

Massimo took the sofa opposite and frowned as he saw the play of emotions on her face, wondering if he had rushed things. She had only hours ago buried her husband. Yes, she had married Joseph Ferliani for money and a lucrative modelling contract, but it was still possible she had developed some feelings for him over the last five years.

But then, he quickly reminded himself, no doubt losing everything she had worked so hard to gain was inducement enough to break down emotionally. He had seen the same crocodile-tears in his mother's eyes when her financial supply had finally dried up. He had learned to ignore such emotional displays, and this time would be no different. Nikki Ferliani was after money and position, for why else had she married his stepfather and stayed married to him for five years?

He watched as she put the menu down, her trembling hand reaching for her purse. She took out a scrunched-up tissue and wiped her eyes before stuffing it back inside and snapping the catch closed.

'You are upset.'

Nikki met his eyes with an ironic look. 'You sound surprised,' she said.

'It has been a hard day for you,' he conceded. 'I have perhaps underestimated just how hard.'

Her expression turned sour. 'Don't try and be nice to me, Massimo, it doesn't suit you any more.'

'If I am not nice it is your fault,' he said in a clipped tone. 'What you did to me was unforgiveable, so do not complain if I do not treat you the way I used to. I am not so naïve and stupid these days.'

'We met at the wrong time,' she said, lowering her gaze from the searing scorn of his.

'I disagree,' he said. 'We met at exactly the right time. I found out before it was too late the lengths some women will go to in order to get themselves a meal ticket. You rejected me and married a man two-and-a-half times your age to land yourself a fortune—a fortune I have great pleasure in reminding you that you no longer possess.'

Nikki's hands tightened on the purse in her lap as she brought her eyes back to his. 'You shouldn't have destroyed him,' she said, with bitterness sharpening every word to a dagger point. 'You shouldn't have humiliated him when he had already suffered for so long.'

A tiny nerve flickered at the side of his mouth. 'You are telling *me* what I should have done or not done?' he asked.

She lifted her chin, her eyes glittering at him rebelliously. 'Yes, I am. You could have bought the business from him at a reduced price instead of rubbing his nose in it the way you did.'

His eyes flashed with sparks of anger. 'I did no less than he did to my father.'

'That's not the point,' she argued. 'What good did it do to go after him? What victory is there in destroying a man who was already dying?'

'It was a matter of honour,' he said through clenched teeth.

'What a pity your modus operandi wasn't always honourable,' she tossed back.

His lip curled. 'You sound as if you really cared about him,' he said.

'Yes…' She caught at her bottom lip for a moment. 'Yes, I did.'

'But you still married him for money, did you not?'

The silence left hanging after his question began to drum in Nikki's ears.

'I married him because I had to,' she said after a long pause.

A small frown appeared between his brows. 'Had to?' he asked, leaning forward slightly. 'What do you mean by that?'

Nikki was momentarily caught off guard. 'Um…I…'

'Did he force you?'

It would have been so easy to tell him the truth, she thought.

But in the long months of nursing Joseph through his terminal illness she had learned much of what had made him act so ruthlessly back then. His childhood had its similarities to hers; the loneliness, rejection and guilt he'd spoken about in his last days of life had stirred her very deeply. To talk of such delicate things with his enemy stepson would seem like a betrayal to her of the tentative trust and companionship that had developed between them. Joseph had been a damaged man, but a good one for all that.

'No,' she said after a tense little pause. 'No, he didn't force me.'

'So you married him because you wanted to do so.'

'Yes,' she said, forcing her eyes to hold his. 'I married him because it was what I wanted to do at the time.'

His dark gaze pinned hers determinedly. 'But you did not love him, or at least not then?'

She let a tiny breath escape from between her lips. 'No…'

Another pulsing silence thickened the air between them.

'Why did you not tell me the first night we met that you were engaged to be married the following weekend?' he asked.

She couldn't hold his penetrating look, and stared down at the clasp on her purse. 'I'm not sure…I thought about it several times, but I wanted to forget and be someone else that night.' She dragged her eyes back to his. 'You didn't meet me that night, or indeed for any part of that week, Massimo. Or at least not the real me.'

'Who is the "real you"?'

How could she tell him who she was? How could she confess to such shame? What would he think, to hear of how as a young child she had rummaged through garbage bins in an effort to find something for Jayden and herself to eat when their mother hadn't been able to cope or had lain injured from yet another beating? Or that from the age of eight she'd had to fight off the inappropriate attentions of her father, lying awake in terror most nights, cuddling Jayden close to her in case her father turned his attention to him instead?

And how would he react to find out the terrible truth about why her brother could no longer feed or toilet himself, his body shattered and slumped in a wheelchair, his once-brilliant mind vacant?

Nikki looked away without answering, her eyes stinging with the acid rain of regret and guilt.

'Who is the woman sitting opposite me now?' Massimo asked. 'Is she the social climbing gold-digger or the girl with the golden heart?'

'What if I am both?' she asked, a fleeting shadow of sadness in her eyes as they returned to his. 'What if I am one and the same?'

The drinks waiter appeared at that moment to take their order, giving Massimo time to reflect on her answer. She was a complicated person; he could see that now. She had depths and layers he had not really noticed in that first week of heady passion. But he was determined to uncover each and every one of them now.

He had waited so long for revenge. He had thought of nothing for five long years. Each punishing day working at building his investment empire had been for this chance to turn the tables on her.

He had been ruthless in his pursuit of wealth and power. His anger towards his stepfather had become almost insignificant as he had planned his revenge on her.

Nikki Ferliani had a reputation for being cool and composed; her ice-maiden looks suggested to him she had nothing but a heart of stone beneath that hot, tempting body.

He was not going to be lured in by her innocent act all over again.

This time he would have her where he wanted her, where he had dreamed of having her for the last five years.

In his bed.

CHAPTER SIX

'MR ANDROLETTI, the table you requested is ready now,' the waiter informed Massimo a short time later.

'Thank you,' Massimo said, and, offering a hand to Nikki, helped her to her feet.

Nikki felt her fingers tingle from the contact with his, but when she tried to remove her hand, his hold tightened.

He looked down at the heavy rings on her wedding finger, his brows coming together over his eyes as he turned the cluster of diamonds to catch the light. His eyes came back to hers, his expression like curtains drawn across a stage. 'Did you enjoy being married to him, Nikki?' he asked.

Nikki hesitated over her answer. It seemed she was caught either way. A 'yes' would incite his anger, but a 'no' would probably provoke him to wonder why she had endured an unhappy marriage, no doubt assuming she had done so in order to maintain her glamorous lifestyle.

'Like any marriage it had its good and bad moments,' she said, trying to remove her hand without success.

'Did he treat you well, Nikki?'

She disguised a small swallow. 'Yes…yes, he did,' she said, lowering her eyes to where their hands were linked.

She felt a tremor of desire brush over the base of her belly as she saw the way his tanned skin contrasted with her creamy smoothness. He had large, square hands with long, slightly blunt fingers, the nails neatly maintained, the dusting of masculine hair making her aware of her femininity in a way she hadn't been in years.

He released her hand and led her by the elbow to their table, where five years ago he had looked at her with desire burning in his eyes.

Nikki sat down and hoped he couldn't see how distressed she was. It was too much. Why had he done this? Surely it was taking revenge too far? So many young people fell in and out of love and moved on with their lives. Why couldn't he? What good was this going to do? It wasn't going to change anything. She had married another man for reasons he would probably never understand. How could anyone understand, unless they had carried the burden of shame as long as she had carried it?

A vision of her young brother's face came to mind and her heart tightened painfully. Jayden was always going to be her top priority. It was the only way she could deal with the tragedy of the past. If she had to go through hell and high water, she would do it.

It was the price she had to pay.

Massimo waited until the waiter had left with their order before he asked, 'Do you still have the ring I gave you?'

Nikki looked at him in confusion. 'I gave it back to you. I left a message with the concierge on duty that there was a package for you to collect. Didn't you receive it?'

His eyes hardened with suspicion. 'No, I did not.'

She chewed at her lower lip, her eyes now downcast.

'I'm sorry you didn't get it back. Someone must have stolen it.'

'I think we both know who that someone was.'

Her head came back up at that, her grey-blue eyes wide with appeal. 'I didn't take it, Massimo. Surely you don't think I would do something like that?'

'You stole my heart,' he said with an embittered look. 'Why shouldn't you steal a ring worth a small fortune as well?'

Nikki felt totally crushed by his cynicism, and yet she knew if the ring hadn't been returned to him he had every right to assume she had taken it. 'I wish we had never met that night,' she said on the tail end of a despondent sigh. 'I wish I had never gone into that bar and gone straight upstairs instead.'

'Why did you?'

Nikki compressed her lips as she thought about it. She had spent the afternoon with her brother in the hospice where he had been placed once she'd no longer been able to manage him at home by herself. The nurses had been incredibly caring and attentive but terribly overworked. They'd done the best they could do, but Jayden needed one-on-one care and instant access to a doctor on twenty-four-hour call. That sort of care came at an astronomical cost that few families could afford for their loved ones.

'I'm taking you out of here soon,' she'd promised him as she'd stroked some warmth into his thin, cold hands. 'I'm going to do everything in my power to make sure you get the best help there is.'

One of the nurses had walked past with a bundle of bedding and gave Nikki a tired smile. 'I hear you've organised a place at Rosedale House for him,' she said. 'That will cost you a pretty penny.'

'Yes,' Nikki said, still holding on to her brother's hand.

The nurse had looked at Jayden and shaken her head. 'It's a tragedy what these young folk do to themselves in fast cars,' she'd said. 'We've got a new admission coming in this afternoon. Motorcycle accident. He's in a similar condition to your brother. There's no way of managing him at home. You can't help feeling sorry for the parents—all that potential gone to waste.'

'Yes,' Nikki had said, feeling another arrow of guilt pierce her heart.

'Well, good luck, then,' the nurse said as she'd moved on.

'Thank you,' Nikki said, and with a sigh had turned back to her brother.

Massimo looked at the bowed figure across the table and frowned. 'You didn't answer my question,' he said. 'Why did you go to the bar?'

She lifted her gaze to meet his. 'I didn't want to be alone that night.'

Something shifted in his chest as he saw the way her small white teeth captured her bottom lip, the slight tremble of her chin making her appear as vulnerable as a small child.

He was annoyed with himself for being affected by her after all this time. It wasn't supposed to happen this way. He was the one in control now. He was the one who was calling the tune for her to dance to, not the other way around. For all he knew, this could be another act of hers to gain sympathy. After all, she was now destitute with a mountain of debts banked up behind her. She was no doubt looking for a way to dig herself permanently out of the mess, by getting him to offer to marry her. But he was not going to be played for a lovesick fool again.

'What would you like for the next course?' He diverted the conversation to less treacherous ground. 'The menu has changed from when we last dined here, of course.'

'I'm surprised you didn't talk the chef into recreating it,' she said with an edge of bitterness sharpening her tone.

'Perhaps I should have done. Although I do not think I would be able to remember what we ate that night.'

'I can,' Nikki said, before she'd stopped to think about what she was actually revealing.

'Oh really?' His brows rose in speculation. 'You have that good a memory?'

A frown pulled at her smooth forehead as she looked away from him. 'For some things, I guess...' she said.

Massimo watched as she toyed with the edge of the tablecloth with her fingers, the movements suggesting an inner restlessness he found faintly intriguing. He would have to be careful around her, he decided. That hint of fragility about her was all an act. She was after security and was prepared to do anything to get it. She had pretended to be outraged at his suggestion that they share his bed, but he had seen the looks she had given him when she hadn't thought he was watching. She had hungry eyes, and not just for money. His groin tightened as he thought about her panting beneath him the way she had that one night in the past.

He gripped the stem of his glass as he thought about her doing the same with his stepfather, her slender body bucking beneath the sweating, overweight bulk of a man who had indulged his every appetite to the extreme.

His gut shuddered, and he shook with nausea. How could she have sold herself in such a despicable way?

He pushed his glass aside before he was tempted to smash it against the nearest wall. 'You and Joseph did not have children,' he said in a tone that belied the true state of his feelings.

Her eyes met his briefly. 'No…'

'His choice or yours?'

Nikki wondered what he would say if she told him she had never once slept with Joseph Ferliani. That had been her condition on agreeing to the marriage, and she had been grateful he had accepted it, and had never once gone back on his word.

'The chemotherapy he had a few months before we married made him infertile,' she said, which was also true. 'It was a great sadness to him that he hadn't been able to have a child.'

'And what about you?' he asked after another tiny pause.

Her eyes were fixed on the glass of water in front of her. 'It wasn't an issue for me,' she said.

'Meaning what, exactly?'

'Meaning I don't want to have children.'

'Any particular reason why?' he asked.

Nikki brought her eyes back to his with an effort. 'I don't think I would make a good mother.'

'What makes you believe that? Was your mother a bad mother?'

'No, of course not,' she said, perhaps a little too quickly.

'But?'

'There's no but,' she said. 'I just don't want to go down that path. It's not for me.'

'There are many who would say that a woman who does not want children is being selfish,' he commented.

'That is a very outdated view,' she countered. 'There are

lots of women who don't see children as an option for their lives. There are plenty of childless men out there, and no one would ever dream of calling them selfish.'

'Point taken,' he said agreeably. 'I had not considered that angle.'

'What about you?' she asked, when she could stand the stretching silence no longer. 'Are you hoping to have children one day?'

'It is something I think about occasionally,' he said. 'I am now thirty-three. At the same age my father had been married for seven years. But for now, I am happy as things are. There are many benefits to being a playboy.'

Nikki ground her teeth, and dearly wished the waiter would hurry up and bring their meals so the evening could be over. She had tried so hard over the years not to think about him with other women. She had mostly succeeded, but now seeing him again had brought it all back to her: what she had experienced that one time in his arms—the magic, the joy and the mind-blowing pleasure.

But he didn't want her in that capacity any longer. She was little more than an employee this time around, a trophy mistress with no real status in his life.

She flicked her napkin across her lap as the waiter approached, and in spite of her lack of appetite she worked her way through the delicious meal in an effort to avoid small talk. But she came to realise after a while, that the sound of her cutlery was making conversation for her. Each cut of a knife or jab of a fork seemed to be saying something of an embittered nature.

'You are angry at your food for some reason?' Massimo asked after she had given the delicate meat on her plate a particularly vicious jab with her fork.

Nikki put the fork down with a little clatter. 'I can't do this,' she said and got to her feet, her eyes glistening with moisture. 'I can't sit here and pretend this isn't affecting me.'

His dark gaze collided with hers. 'Sit down, Nikki.'

Her blue-grey eyes tussled with his for a long moment, but then, blowing out a breath of resignation, she sat back down. 'I'm sorry,' she said, looking down at her plate, her shoulders sagging. 'I'm not used to being in public any more. I feel a bit exposed. It's been a while since I've eaten out.'

Massimo reached across the table and took one of her hands in the warmth of his. 'Perhaps, I should not have brought you here. Not today. You are grieving. I did not realise you would be so affected by my stepfather's passing.' *Or by his leaving you destitute*, he said under his breath as he gauged her reaction.

She bit at her lip for a moment, releasing it to say in a subdued tone, 'It was so hard those last few weeks. I know you probably think he deserved it, but I hated seeing him suffer. He was such a big man, and yet he faded away to nothing...' A tear escaped from the corner of her eye and she brushed at it with the back of her hand. 'I'm not usually so emotional. Over the years I've taught myself to keep it inside.'

'That surely cannot be a good thing,' he said, absently stroking her soft palm with his thumb.

'No.' She gave a serrated sigh. 'No...I guess not.'

Massimo gave her hand a little squeeze. 'Come, I will take you home.'

She lifted her reddened eyes to his. 'Are you sure?'

He gave a nod as he helped her to her feet. 'I am not enjoying the meal either.' *Or by being taken for the biggest fool this side of the Nullarbor,* he felt like adding. God, but she was good at this stuff. She had it down to a science—the tears, the despair, even the tiny tremble of her small chin was startlingly realistic. But he hardened his heart as he led her outside. She hadn't yet met with the lawyer, and when she did he could almost predict what would happen. She would learn her financial status and there would be no 'I don't want to sleep with you' statements then, he was sure.

Nikki followed him out to the waiting car and sat silently beside him as they made the short journey to South Yarra, her emotions still seesawing inside her. Being in Massimo's presence disturbed her so deeply. Every time he looked at her she felt his scorn and hatred, when five years ago nothing but melting softness had shone from those eyes.

'I will walk you to the door,' he said as Ricardo pulled into the driveway.

'No, please don't bother,' she said, suddenly desperate to be alone. 'I'll be fine.'

'It is of no bother to me, and besides I would like to see the house I now own.'

Nikki pulled her mouth tight at his imperious tone. 'All right, then. Come this way.'

She walked stiffly to the door and, unlocking it, stepped aside for him to enter. 'Make yourself at home,' she said with a little pointed look.

He moved past her and took his time looking around the lower floor, stopping here and there to inspect a painting on the wall or an object on display.

After what seemed an age, he came back to where she was standing, his gaze taking in her tightly crossed arms and hard expression. 'It is just a house, Nikki,' he said. 'And not a particularly beautiful one.'

'It's not just a house,' she bit out. 'It's my home.' The first she had ever had, in fact. Sure, it wasn't exactly to her taste, but she had loved the privacy and security it offered.

'Not any more, it isn't,' he reminded her.

She gave him an embittered glare. 'No, because you won't be happy until you have total control over me, will you?'

He took her chin between his thumb and index finger, tilting her head so she locked gazes with him. 'Can you blame me for wanting it all?' he asked.

'You're going too far. You know you are. You practically admitted it yourself this evening.'

His eyes dropped to her mouth. 'I do not think I have taken things far enough,' he said, his thumb moving from her chin to press against the soft contours of her bottom lip.

Nikki swallowed against the ground swell of feeling that his simple touch evoked. 'Don't,' she said raggedly. 'Please, don't…'

His mouth came close enough for her to feel the brush of his warm breath on her lips. 'You do not want me to kiss you, Nikki?' he asked softly.

'No,' she breathed as her mouth inched closer to his almost of its own volition. 'No, I don't…'

'Do you not need to be reminded of what it felt like to have my tongue playing with yours?' he asked.

She moistened her lips. 'No…'

'So you have not forgotten, eh, Nikki?' he said, brushing the seam of her mouth with the tip of his tongue.

Her legs swayed beneath her, and she had to clutch at him for stability. 'No, I haven't forgotten a thing,' she said on the back of a shaky sigh.

'Nor have I,' he said and brought his mouth down on hers.

Nikki felt her mouth explode with the burning heat of his, the first entry of his tongue making her toes curl inside her shoes. Her body came to instant life, energy racing like a current of electricity through the intricate network of her veins as his hands slid down her hips to pull her closer.

The hot, hard heat of him against her pelvis sent her pulse soaring; she could even feel her heart slamming against her sternum as he deepened the kiss even further.

Her breasts peaked and swelled against his chest, her belly giving a quick, hard kick of excitement when one of his hands left her hip to move upwards to cup the fullness of her breast. She pressed herself closer, her body acting of its own accord in a desperate need to feel more of his possessive touch.

His mouth ground against hers with increasing fervour, as if the fire he had set alight in her body had now spread to his. She felt it in the bruising pressure of his kiss, felt it too in the hard thrust of his tongue in its quest to subdue hers, and she heard it in the deep groan that came from the back of his throat, as her hands moved to cup his taut buttocks to keep him tightly locked against her.

His tongue flicked against hers, coiling, sweeping and conquering, until she could barely stand upright. She felt the graze of his teeth against her swollen bottom lip, and she began to nip at him in tiny tug-and-release bites that brought another deep, guttural groan from his throat.

Suddenly it was over.

He stepped back from her without warning, leaving her stranded in a swirling sea of unmet needs. She opened her eyes and blinked, feeling disoriented and dishevelled, and, when she encountered his cold, hard gaze, deeply ashamed, as well.

'It seems I was right. You are indeed very keen to find a

replacement for your dead husband after all,' he said with a mocking look.

Pride brought her chin up. 'I think it's time you left,' she said.

'You cannot order me from my own house, *cara*,' he said. 'If I choose to stay then I will stay.'

'I hate you for what you're doing to me,' she said with a fulminating glare.

'Hate is good, Nikki. I prefer that to the lies about love you spoke of five years ago.'

'I never told you I loved you,' she said, doing her best to avoid his eyes. 'You were the one who read more into the relationship than what was there.'

'You cold-hearted little slut,' he ground out viciously. 'You love money and position, not people. You will do anything to get it, won't you? I bet if I had offered to give you this house back you would have let me take you right here where we are standing.'

She turned away so he wouldn't see the tears she was desperately trying to hold back. 'Please leave,' she said in a strangled voice. '*Please*…just go.'

'I will see you tomorrow at my house as arranged,' he said into the brittle silence. 'I will send Ricardo to fetch you. And I think I should advise you against reneging on the deal. You have too much to lose.'

I have already lost it all, Nikki thought once the door had slammed on his exit. She laid her head back against the nearest wall and groaned. *Dear God; I have already lost it all.*

CHAPTER SEVEN

'YOU mean it's true?' Nikki gasped in shock. 'There's really nothing left? Nothing at all?'

Joseph's lawyer, Peter Rozzoli, shook his head. 'I'm sorry, Mrs Ferliani,' he said, his tone anything but apologetic. 'Your late husband left things in an awful mess. I know things got tough towards the end for him, but he really should have organised someone to run things for him when he no longer could manage it.'

Nikki couldn't help feeling the lawyer was laying the blame for that at her door. She'd never really liked the man on the few occasions Joseph had invited him to the house. It had seemed to her he was always looking at her in a predatory manner, but whenever she'd mentioned it to Joseph he had just laughed, and said Peter was jealous of him having such a beautiful young wife.

'Joseph told me everything was going well,' she said, in her defence. 'I asked him numerous times.'

'Joseph as you know was a very proud man,' the lawyer said. 'The way he handled his illness was a case in point. No one would have ever believed he'd been fighting cancer for so long.'

She looked down at the papers on the desk between them and swallowed. 'I can't believe he left things like this,' she said. 'I have bills and…and expenses.'

The prolonged silence brought her head back up to meet a gaze not dissimilar from the one she had spent most of the previous day avoiding.

'You will have to find yourself another rich husband or a very wealthy benefactor, and fast, Mrs Ferliani,' Peter Rozzoli said, his snake-like gaze slithering all over her. 'Otherwise you are going to be held responsible for several-hundred thousand dollars' worth of debt.'

Nikki gathered her bag from the floor and stood up on legs that threatened to give way. 'Thank you for your time,' she said stiffly.

The lawyer gave her a nod without rising to his feet. 'Good luck, Mrs Ferliani,' he said. 'But then, from what I read in this morning's paper, you seem to have already landed on your feet.'

Nikki didn't stay around to ask him what he meant. She closed the door on her exit and, taking a ragged little breath, made her way outside.

There was a news stand on the corner near the lawyer's offices, and she almost stumbled when she saw the billboard advertising the story of the day:

BANKRUPT WIDOW ONE DAY—WEALTHY MISTRESS THE NEXT.

She didn't stop to purchase the paper; she didn't need to read the rest for she knew it wouldn't be pretty. The tall-poppy syndrome, so active in the Australian press, had stung her on previous occasions. It went with the territory of being in the public eye. She had only to turn up at an event with a frown and it was reported she was a surly prima donna, or smile too brightly and be accused of being shallow. She had long given up worrying about it, assuring herself that as soon as she could she would toss it all in. But with Joseph leaving things as he had, her plans for a return to anonymity were going to have to be shelved.

She made her way back to Joseph's house on leaden legs, her stomach rolling in panic. She had so wanted to throw Massimo's offer in his face. She had allowed him to think she was agreeing to it, but she had been desperately hoping he had somehow been misinformed about Joseph's finances.

It didn't seem possible things had gone so badly without her knowing. She had spent long months nursing Joseph, holding his gaunt body as he was sick, bathing him, spooning what little food she could into his mouth, and yet he had said nothing. He had instead assured her things were all in order and she would have no money worries in the future. She wasn't sure what hurt the most—the fact that he had lied to her, or that she had been foolish enough to believe him.

Massimo was waiting for her in the study of his house when she arrived with Ricardo later that morning. He looked up from his desk and asked her to take a seat. 'There are some things I need to ask you about the business,' he said.

'I'm not sure I will be able to help you with any of that,' she said, briefly capturing her bottom lip. 'In the last few months I had less and less to do with things. You'd be better to speak to Kenneth Slade, the business manager.'

'I have already spoken to him. In fact, I have spoken with

everyone in the company,' he said. 'They seemed to think I should talk to you.'

Nikki sat very still, but her hands twitched in her lap no matter how hard she tried to stop them.

'I was not aware until very recently that you took over the designing of the spring-summer collection when my stepfather became too ill to meet the deadlines,' he said. 'The designs are some of the best I have ever seen.'

She met his eyes briefly, unable to disguise her surprise at his compliment. 'Thank you.'

'It seems you have a natural flair,' he went on. 'Which is what I wanted to talk to you about this morning.'

Nikki rolled her lips together, not sure where this was leading. 'I see…'

She heard the creak of leather as he leaned back in his chair, and she chanced a look at him. His dark gaze was watching her steadily, but his expression was as mask-like as ever which made her feel even more uneasy.

'Are you interested in being contracted for the next autumn-winter collection?' he asked.

She blinked at him. 'You're…you're offering me a job?'

'I gave you a job yesterday, if you remember,' he said with another unfathomable look.

She sent the tip of her tongue out to her lips, running it over the dryness in an agitated gesture. 'Yes, I realise that, but I meant another job on top of *that* one…'

'Yes,' he said as his chair creaked again. 'I am offering you another job. Are you interested?'

She pressed her damp palms to her knees and met his eyes. 'Yes, I am interested,' she said. 'But only if you are prepared to pay me well.'

One of his dark brows came up in a perfect arc over one cynical eye. 'I take it you have consulted your husband's lawyer?' he said as he began to toy with his pen.

'I have been informed of the state of affairs, yes,' she answered.

'You are shocked by what you heard?'

'Of course,' she said, looking at him instead of the movement of his pen in his fingers. 'I am very shocked that I seem to have been the last person to find out how bad things had got.'

He tossed the pen to one side and sent a raking gaze over her designer outfit. 'You were probably too busy spending the money to know where it was coming from, or whether or not it was likely to dry up,' he said. 'That was your job after all, wasn't it, Nikki? To act the dumb blonde, the sexy little wife, to see to your older husband's needs in exchange for the wealth and position he could provide.'

Nikki ground her teeth until her jawed ached. 'I was a good wife to your stepfather,' she bit out. 'And money had nothing to do with it.'

He got to his feet so suddenly she felt the rush of air from his movement against her face. He slammed his fist down on the desk between them, his eyes twin pools of black fury.

'You are nothing, but a cheap little slut,' he said. 'You sit here, telling me you were a good wife, when you were flirting with everything in trousers behind my stepfather's back.'

Nikki stared at him in shock. 'That's not true!'

He pushed himself away from the desk, his expression full of disdain. 'Your husband's lawyer told me how you tried to come on to him every time he came to the house.'

Her jaw dropped open, and it took her far too long to find

her voice. 'Peter Rozzoli is a *liar*!' She practically shrieked the words at him as she got to her feet. 'He's a sleazy, double-tongued snake who I've never trusted in all the years he's worked for Joseph. It wouldn't surprise me if he had something to do with the business failing the way it did.'

'What was the problem, Nikki?' he asked with a sardonic tilt of his mouth. 'Didn't he offer you enough to have an affair with him?'

Nikki had to curl her fingers into her palm to stop herself from slapping his arrogant face. 'No amount of money would have tempted me to get involved with him,' she said. 'Besides, he's married.'

'Ah, but you are prepared to do business with me,' he said as he closed the distance between them.

Nikki's startled gaze flicked sideways to instinctively check for an escape route, her heart missing a beat when she couldn't see one. She held her breath as he cupped her cheek with his palm, her eyes unable to avoid the smouldering intensity of his.

'But I am not married, am I, Nikki?' he said, his thumb roving over the curve of her cheek in a slow, imminently sensual motion.

'I-I'm not interested,' she said, pushing his hand away from her face with what little willpower she had left.

He gave her a cool smile. 'We will see,' he said as he returned to his chair behind the desk. 'You have not had long enough to realise how dire your situation is. When you do, I can almost guarantee you will seek refuge in my bed.'

Nikki sat down again only because her legs were refusing to hold her up. 'I thought you wanted to discuss business with me,' she said with a frosty look. 'If that's not the case, then I would like to leave.'

He held her hostile glare for a lengthy moment before announcing, 'I would like you to accompany me to Sicily to look over the garment factory.'

She jerked upright in her seat. 'Sicily?'

His brows lifted again. 'I would have thought you of all people would not be uncomfortable with the notion of travelling abroad,' he said. 'You went everywhere with my stepfather did you not?'

'Not for the last year,' she said, lowering her eyes again.

'Perhaps it is the notion of travelling with me that is the problem, eh, Nikki?' he said, his tone containing a thin, but unmistakable thread of anger.

Her eyes came back to his. 'I am prepared to pretend to be your mistress, but I wouldn't want you to get any ideas about making fiction turn into fact.'

He gave her another cold smile. 'You are very sure of yourself, are you not?'

She refused to answer, and instead sat silently glaring at him.

He leaned back in his chair once more, his pen tapping against the edge of the desk as he observed her. 'You are reeling me in, aren't you, Nikki?' he asked. 'Making me want you all over again. Every look you give me, every flutter of your lashes, and every movement of your tongue across your lips, is all part of your plan to have me make you a permanent fixture in my life.'

'You're imagining it,' she said crisply. 'No doubt because you're so used to women falling over themselves to dive into your bed.'

'Are you going to deny the attraction you still feel for me?' he asked.

Nikki felt the force field of his gaze as it tugged hers back to his, her body tingling all over when his eyes roved over her in male appraisal. She felt the tightening of her breasts, her nipples going to hard little points as if he had brushed them with his lips and tongue as he done so passionately in the past. She clamped her thighs together to stop the rush of liquid longing, but it was a useless exercise; her whole body quivered with the memory of his hard possession, and she was almost certain he knew it.

'Of course I'm going to deny it,' she said. 'I have no interest in any sort of relationship with you.'

He ignored her denial to inform her, 'I have organised our flights for Friday morning. We will spend a week at my villa. I thought after the article in this morning's paper you would be glad of a temporary reprieve.'

Nikki felt her stomach go hollow all over again. 'I haven't read the paper this morning. I took one look at the billboard and decided it wasn't worth it.'

He unfolded the newspaper he had on the desk and handed it to her. 'I should warn you, it is not a very flattering piece of journalism,' he said.

She looked down at the photo taken at Joseph's funeral the day before. The photographer had captured her smiling at the sales manager. It was just a tiny moment in time, and yet the journalist had used it to portray her as a shallow, money-hungry widow who was apparently rejoicing in the demise of her husband.

The article went on to describe her as the latest lover of Italian investment tycoon Massimo Androletti, the new owner of Ferliani Fashions, the journalist even speculating that their affair had been going on behind Joseph Ferliani's back as he'd struggled with terminal cancer.

Nikki tossed the paper down in disgust, her rage directed at Massimo as she got agitatedly to her feet. 'You did this, didn't you?' she blasted him. 'You fed them a pack of lies to make me look like an immoral tart—*didn't you?*'

He gave her a look of implacable calm, which in the presence of her anger made her all the more furious. 'You know what journalists are like, *cara*,' he said. 'They make these things up to ramp up sales.'

She slammed her hand on the desk, her chest heaving as she leaned towards him. '*You* made it up to send a message to your stupid ex-mistress, but you couldn't resist embellishing it to make me appear as tacky and tasteless as possible, could you?'

His gaze travelled lazily to the hint of cleavage she was showing, before returning to her glittering eyes. 'I did no such thing. I am always extremely careful in what I reveal to the press. However, it is perhaps rather unfortunate timing—but as I said, this trip away will allow the dust to settle.'

'*Unfortunate timing?*' she spluttered at him. 'As far as I can see you've timed it to a second, turning up at the funeral like that, issuing your demands like the overbearing tyrant you are.'

'I have already spoken to you about your tendency to speak incautiously when addressing me, Nikki,' he warned her silkily as he got to his feet.

Nikki had to fight with every instinct not to step backwards as he came from behind the desk. She stood stock still, her hands clenched by her sides, her greyish-blue eyes flashing with anger. 'I never thought I'd say this, but I hate you, Massimo Androletti. Do you hear me? I hate you.'

A nerve pulsed like a tiny jackhammer beneath the skin of

his jaw, his gaze black as night as it speared hers. 'You can hate me all you like whilst in the confines of this house, but as soon as we leave it you will have to abide by the rules I lay down— otherwise you will find yourself with legal bills that will take you years to read through, much less pay.'

He took his car keys out of his trouser pocket and added, 'I am going to my office in the city. I will be home for dinner at approximately seven-thirty.'

'If you think I'm going to cook a meal and wait for you to return to eat it you've definitely got rocks in your head,' she said. 'If you're not here on time, I'll toss it in the bin.'

'La mia piccola padrona arrabbiata,' he said, with a mocking little smile. '"My angry little mistress".'

She glared at him heatedly. 'Don't call me that.'

'Would you prefer *"la mia padrona, piccola e cara"*?' he asked. 'That is what you are, is it not, Nikki? My *dear* little mistress—for I have paid a lot of money for you.'

She could feel her teeth turning to powder as she clenched her jaw. 'You don't own me.'

He flicked her cheek with the end of one long finger. 'Ah, but I do,' he said, his voice a deep, velvet drawl. 'And when the time is ready, I will take what you have to offer.'

'I'm offering you nothing.'

His dark eyes glinted. 'That was not the impression I got from you last night,' he said.

'Last night was a mistake,' she threw back. 'I wasn't myself. I was upset and overly emotional. And you took advantage of it.'

'I only took advantage of what was going begging,' he returned, neatly. 'And if it is ever on offer again, I will do the very same. You have taught me well, eh, Nikki? I do not wear my heart on my sleeve any more. Once was more than enough.'

'You can't blame me for ever for your own limitations,' she said. 'You have a choice to behave in an honourable way, in spite of what may have happened to you in the past.'

'You speak to me of honour when you have prostituted yourself for five years to a man old enough to be your father?' he snarled. 'Seeing you on his arm the day of the wedding sickened me to my stomach, when only the night before you had been sobbing in my arms in ecstasy.'

She put her hands to her ears to block the sound of his words. 'Stop it!'

He pulled her hands away and carried on in the same angry, bitter tone, 'Did he make you scream when you came, Nikki? Did he make you so desperate for release you raked his back with your nails? *Did he?*'

'No!'

'You lie!' He threw the words at her. 'He held you on his arm like a trophy at every opportunity he could. I saw the photographs in the press. He was smiling like a cat who had stolen the cream. But it was *my* cream, wasn't it, Nikki? It still is, and you and I both know it. Last night proved it.'

'I am no man's possession,' she said, trying to get out of his hold. 'And certainly not yours.'

He refused to release her, his fingers biting into the flesh of her upper arms. 'I still want you and I intend to have you,' he said. 'It is only a matter of time.'

'I am *not* going to sleep with you.' Nikki hoped by saying it enough times it would somehow make it true.

'You will not be able to help yourself,' he said. 'I see the longing in your eyes every time you look at me.'

'You're imagining it. I feel nothing where you're concerned.'

He smiled tauntingly as he pulled her even closer so she
could feel where his body burned and throbbed against her.
'You are feeling it now, aren't you, Nikki? The same burning
desire we've felt for each other from the moment we met.'

Nikki could feel her body betraying her, every pore of her
skin aching with the need to feel his touch. She couldn't think
with the temptation of his mouth so close to hers, the jut of
his hard body reminding her of the passion they had once
shared. Her inner core tightened and melted simultaneously,
like a secret pulse deep inside her body, where his had once
moved with such strength and virile potency.

'I don't want you,' she said even as her mouth lifted to meet
the descent of his. 'I don't want—'

His mouth cut off the rest of her pointless denial, his
tongue delving into her moist warmth to meet hers in a sexy
tango that sent shivers of reaction up and down her spine. Her
limbs turned to liquid as he deepened the kiss even further,
exploring every corner of her mouth with almost savage
intent.

His evening shadow scored her soft skin as he tilted her
head for better access, the sexy rasp inciting her to return his
kiss with a wild abandon that made a mockery of everything
she had said only seconds previously.

She wanted him.

Of course she wanted him.

She had never stopped wanting him, and loving him and
missing him, aching for him and wishing things had been
different.

But he was after revenge, not love, she reminded herself.

He wanted to right the wrongs of the past, but on his terms this time around. She could already guess how it was going to go. He would be the one to walk away when it was over, leaving her as devastated as he had been five years ago.

For a brief moment she considered telling him why she had done what she had done, but knew it wouldn't really change anything. He had hated Joseph Ferliani and all he represented. Telling him how his stepfather had helped her escape from her background would no doubt only incense him further. He would argue that Joseph had used money that wasn't his to gain her favour. And a small part of her had to admit he was right. She would never have married Joseph if he hadn't offered her money. Money had been her passport out of her past, and a way to give some measure of comfort to Jayden. And she had clutched at it with both hands, grateful that Joseph had never once asked why she had needed it.

However, Nikki knew that, even if by some miracle Massimo still felt something for her after all this time, learning about her background would surely kill it. He was a high-profile man, with investment clients from all over the world. Having a wife with a background such as hers would be the death knell of their relationship. If word got out in the press that the woman he was involved with was the daughter of one of Australia's most violent criminals, what would it do to his reputation?

With a superhuman effort she pulled back from his hold, pressing both of her hands against his chest to separate their bodies. 'No,' she said. 'This is all wrong.'

'What is wrong about fulfilling a need that we both share?' he asked.

'I can't do this, Massimo,' she said, so close to tears she

had to bite the inside of her mouth until she tasted the metallic sourness of blood.

'Because it is too soon?' he asked.

'Because it is *wrong*,' she said. 'Can't you see that? You hate me.'

He stepped away from her, his hand raking a jagged pathway through his hair as he turned his back on her. 'Perhaps you are right,' he said heavily. 'Hate and desire can be a lethal mix.'

'You have to let it go, Massimo. We had a past, but it's over. I admit I was wrong in leading you on to believe we had the chance of a future together, but I was young, and…and I had already made a promise to your stepfather.'

He turned to face her, his expression sharpened again by bitterness. 'You could have told him you had met someone else,' he said. 'Why didn't you?'

She swallowed against the lump of pain in her throat. 'I had already made a commitment to him. He had given me money, a lot of money, that I had already spent. I know it sounds horribly mercenary to you, but I was in trouble and needed his money to get out of it.'

'I could have given you money. Why didn't you ask me?'

'You told me you were still building your business,' she said. 'I could read between the lines enough to know you couldn't have given me the amount I needed.'

'What sort of trouble were you in?'

She shifted her gaze from the unwavering probe of his, glad she had already rehearsed her lie with Joseph. 'I was irresponsible over money,' she said. 'It happens to a lot of young people when they first get issued with credit cards. I suddenly owed more than I could handle.'

Massimo wanted to believe her. Everything in him wanted her to be the girl he had met five years ago, but something warned him about falling yet again for her doe-eyed innocence.

'Did you know who I was that week we were together?' he asked after a short, but tense silence.

Her eyes came back to his. 'No...no, I didn't, but I should have,' she said, snagging her bottom lip with her teeth for a moment. 'When I thought about it later there were so many connections I could have made, but for some reason I ignored them. I just wanted that week to be about us—two young people who had briefly fallen in love.'

'But you were not in love with me, though, were you?' he asked. 'For if you were you would not have married my stepfather.'

'You don't get it, do you?' she said, her tone bordering on despair. 'Sometimes in life, things go against your best-laid plans. I had responsibilities that I couldn't get out of, I had no choice. You have to accept that. I would do the same again.'

'Then you really are the coldhearted gold-digger I thought you were after all,' he said. 'You walked away without a backward glance, not even having the decency to tell me to my face that it was over.'

'I left you a note with your ring,' she said. 'I tried to explain as best I could why I couldn't see you again.'

'But I did not get the note or the ring, which makes me start to wonder if you had even left one,' he said. 'You sound so convincing—even those sparkling tears are worthy of an acting award—but I am not a fool, Nikki. I know what you are up to. You have had the financial rug you clung to so greedily ripped from under your feet. I can see the little plan you are hatching.'

'There's no plan. I just—'

'Of *course* there is a plan,' he interrupted her angrily. 'I can see it unfolding before my very eyes. What better way than to make me want you again until I am nearly mad with it? That is how it works, is it not? You want me to be so desperate for you I will agree to keep you in the manner to which you have been accustomed.'

'That's not true. I don't want anything from you.'

A five-second silence drummed in her ears until he broke it by saying, 'What if I said I would do it?' He paused, as if gauging her reaction. 'What if I said that instead of being a trophy mistress, I wanted you to be a real one?'

Nikki stood very still, her blue-grey gaze locked on his, her heart beginning to hammer so loudly she was sure he was able to hear it. She moistened her mouth, but it made no difference; her lips felt like ancient parchment as she moved them to speak in a cracked whisper of sound that didn't even come close to sounding like her voice. 'You don't mean that. You can't possibly mean that...'

He held her gaze for interminable seconds before lowering his mouth to hers in a brief, hard kiss. 'I will see you tonight.'

Nikki didn't even realise she had been holding her breath until the door closed on his exit. She pinched the bridge of her nose as tightly as she could to control the tears, but in silence they came, as if they had been waiting for this moment for years...

CHAPTER EIGHT

ONCE Nikki had spent most of the day unpacking her things in the bedroom she wandered out into the garden, her nostrils instantly flaring as the sharp, lemony fragrance of daphne drifted towards her. The garden was awash with colour, the crimson and pinks of azaleas and rhododendrons, as well as the delicate cream and white of camellias interspersed with the vivid electric-blue of cinerarias.

The verdant lawn was fringed by old beech and elm trees, their new spring-growth tipping their craggy limbs. The air was fresh and cool, the damp, earthy smell reminding her that, typical of Melbourne's weather, winter was not quite ready to move aside for the warmth of spring.

A small, black cat suddenly jumped down from the back fence and came over to her and began to weave its way around her legs, its deep, contented purr clearly audible.

Nikki bent down to stroke the silky black fur. 'Why, hello there, little puss. What's your name, I wonder?' She turned the tinkling identification tag over to find the name 'Pia' engraved there.

'Hello, Pia,' she said. 'I wonder who you belong to.'

The little cat meowed and bumped its head against her

hand. Nikki felt a smile tug at her mouth. 'I am pleased to meet you too, Pia,' she said. 'Do you live nearby?'

The cat trotted towards the back door of the house, stopping occasionally to check to see if Nikki was following.

'You want me to feed you?' Nikki asked. 'I'm not sure if Massimo will appreciate having a neighbour's cat come wandering into his house. But he's not home, and I won't tell if you don't.'

The little cat meowed again and darted indoors.

Nikki found a saucer and poured some milk into it, and watched indulgently as the little pink tongue lapped at it enthusiastically. She searched through the pantry and found a tin of tuna, and, taking out another saucer, forked some onto it and laid it beside the milk.

Once the cat was finished it sat and began to lick its paws, wiping each soft pad over its face before beginning all over again.

'What is it about girls and grooming?' Nikki asked with a wry smile.

The cat blinked at her for a moment before resuming her ablutions, and then after she was finished she jumped up on one of the kitchen chairs, curled into a ball and closed her eyes.

Nikki began to prepare dinner, somehow feeling better now that she had a companion. She even found herself talking to Pia as if she was a friend. 'I've never had a pet before, or at least not one I was ever allowed to keep for longer than a few weeks,' she said as she took out some vegetables from the refrigerator.

'My parents moved so many times when I was growing up, I would no sooner make friends with the local kids and we'd be off again. I was always lonely, the odd one out, the kid with the wrong clothes or shoes, or unkempt hair.'

The cat opened both eyes and blinked at her. Nikki gave her a twisted look and continued, 'Do you realise you're the first person I've ever told that to?'

The cat got down from the chair and came across and rubbed against her legs. 'I didn't even tell Joseph,' Nikki said on a little sigh.

'I told you I never want to hear that name mentioned again in my house,' Massimo said from the door.

Nikki spun around in shock, her heart leaping to her throat. 'I didn't hear you come in,' she said, her face feeling warm.

His eyes went to the cat still twining itself around Nikki's legs. 'So you've met our little neighbour Pia,' he observed.

'Yes…' Nikki said, wondering how much he had heard. She couldn't tell from his expression; if anything he seemed much more interested in the cat, who was now heading towards his long trouser-clad legs.

The cat began nudging his hand when he bent down to stroke her. 'You are a naughty little kitten,' he chided her affectionately. 'How many times have you been told to stay in your own garden, eh?'

Nikki watched in fascination as he picked up the cat and held it to his chest, his free hand stroking its head while its slanted green eyes closed in blissful contentment, the deep purring reverberating in the silence.

'I found her in the garden,' she explained. 'She seemed pretty keen to come inside. She was looking for food. I hope I did the right thing by feeding her.'

Massimo met her slightly anxious gaze. 'It is fine,' he said. 'She belongs to Mrs Lockwood over the back. Her husband has been in the hospital for several weeks, so she is away visiting him for most of the day. Little Pia here gets lonely.'

Yeah, well, I know all about that, Nikki thought, but then she became aware of his deepening scrutiny, and to cover her vulnerability she found herself saying in a resentful tone, 'You're home earlier than you said. I hope you don't expect dinner to be ready. I have barely started.'

His dark eyes glinted. 'You are sounding distinctly wasp-ish, Nikki. Has your day been a particularly unpleasant one?'

She pursed her mouth. 'No more than usual. I met with a sleazy lawyer first thing, then I read a pack of lies about my-self in the paper, unpacked my things in the spare bedroom of a man who hates me, and talked to a black cat all after-noon,' she said. 'Pretty average, really.'

A smile began to lift the edges of his mouth at her dry tone. The cat jumped from his arms to the floor with a soft little thud that sounded loud in the silence.

'You are looking for more excitement, are you, *cara*?' he asked, stepping towards her.

Nikki stood her ground, determined to show she wasn't in-timidated by him, but even so her legs felt weak all of a sud-den. 'What do you think you are doing?' she asked as he put his hands to her waist.

'What do you think I am doing, Nikki?'

She fought back the urge to swallow. 'I don't know, but if it's got anything to do with revisiting our past relationship, you'd better stop right now.'

'You do not like the thought of having my body hot and hard inside yours, eh, Nikki?' he asked, brushing his body against her suggestively. 'Remember how hot and hard I was for you that night we were together? I am almost exploding now, just thinking about it.'

This time she did swallow, a great, big gulping swallow that she couldn't control in time. 'I don't like the idea of making this farcical arrangement between us any more complicated than it already is,' she said a little breathlessly.

He smiled as he looked down at her. 'You are already weakening,' he said. 'I can feel it in your body. You are fighting something bigger than both of us, *cara*. We met five years ago and the passion was uncontrollable.' One of his hands went to where her heart was kicking against her chest wall. 'It is still beating inside of you.'

'D-don't do this, Massimo.'

'Don't do what?' he asked, doing it. His lips brushed against hers, his hand against her heart moving to cup her breast.

Nikki couldn't control the urge to respond to the next soft brush against her mouth. Her lips clung to his, her body tilting towards him, her stiff arms loosening as they moved from her sides to wrap around his solid warmth. She closed her eyes as his mouth covered hers, the first stroke and glide of his tongue against hers making her whimper in rapturous delight.

She felt herself being swept away on a tide of longing that no solid sandbag of commonsense could ever hope to restrain. The kiss became frantic, almost savage, as if the last five years of separation had fuelled his desire for her to an unmanageable level. His teeth scraped against hers, his tongue dived and thrust, and his hands possessed the lush prize of her breasts with greedy intent.

'I have waited for this moment for so long,' he growled against her mouth as he ripped her blouse open, his warm, open palm covering her breast as he pushed her bra out of the way. 'I have never forgotten how you responded to me that night. In all these years no one has even come close.'

She began to paw at his clothes, her fingers as urgent as his as she accessed his chest, her mouth pressing against the base of his throat, her tongue tasting the salt of his skin. She heard him groan as her mouth went to the hard pebble of his right nipple, nestling in amongst the sprinkling of masculine hair that marked him as a man. She had often dreamed of kissing her way down his body. She had been too shy in the past, but the urge to do so now was almost uncontrollable. She wanted to taste him in the most intimate way possible, to feel his explosive release, to show him she had grown from a girl to a woman.

His body was taut as a trip wire beneath her fingertips, his every response to her touch leaving her in no doubt of his ongoing desire for her.

'We cannot do this here,' he said, pulling away from her to look down at her with passion-glazed eyes. 'I want to pleasure you, not against the kitchen bench, but in my bed where you belong.'

Nikki began to extricate herself from his hold, his words reminding her of the reason for her being here. For him this wasn't about a love that hadn't died, it was about revenge.

'No,' she said, pushing against his chest.

'You know you do not mean that, *cara*,' he said, holding her hands against him so she couldn't remove them. 'You want me, but you want me to beg, don't you?'

'I want you to let me go.'

'Ask nicely.'

She gritted her teeth, her eyes flashing with anger. 'Let me go, you arrogant beast.'

He shook his head at her in reproof. 'That is not the way a lover should speak to her partner, Nikki. I hope you did not speak to my stepfather in such a way.'

'Your stepfather was twice the man you are,' she threw back. 'At least he had a conscience.'

His eyes hardened into chips of black ice. 'Oh, really?' he said, dropping his hands from hers. 'Does that mean he confessed his sins on his death bed?'

'He told me he had some regrets over the way he took your father's money from him,' she said as she rebuttoned her top with shaking fingers. 'But your mother was just as much to blame. She encouraged him to take it, insisting it was half hers.'

His lip curled. 'What a pity he didn't apologise to my father at the time. Maybe then my father might still be alive.'

'He was devastated by your father's suicide,' she said. 'It was what, in the end, broke up his relationship with your mother. He felt so guilty.'

Massimo gave a harsh bark of mocking laughter. 'He really did a good job on you, didn't he? Guilty indeed. That low-life creep never suffered a moment's remorse for destroying my father.'

'You didn't know him, not the way I did,' Nikki argued. 'If you had taken the time to get to know him, you might have realised what made him the man he was.'

'I suppose he gave you some sob story about his tortured childhood, did he?' he asked. 'I have no time for people who use that as an excuse. He was no victim, he was a perpetrator.'

Nikki drew in an unsteady breath. 'You don't think a person's childhood has an impact on who they are as adults?'

'I think my stepfather pulled the wool over your eyes, that's what I think,' he said. 'But then maybe the amount he was paying to have you in his bed made you see him through rose-coloured glasses.'

She gave him a flinty look. 'I did not sleep with your stepfather for money.' *I didn't sleep with him at all.*

His expression showed his scepticism in every sharp angle and line of his face. 'Maybe that is what you are hanging out for now,' he said, with an insolent slide of his gaze over her body. 'Am I not paying you enough, eh, Nikki?'

Nikki loathed violence, having grown up with it for most of her life, but she had to keep her hands pinned by her sides as the urge to slap him became almost uncontrollable. 'I am glad I rejected you when I did,' she said through tight lips. 'Joseph might not have been an angel, but he never once insulted me the way you have done.'

A flash of rage lit his eyes as they held hers. 'I think you are more than a little bit ahead of me in the insult stakes, *cara*. You will have to forgive me if I take every opportunity to level the score.'

'You never used to be so cold and calculating. How can you live with yourself?'

'Do not speak to me of being cold and calculating,' he growled. 'You are the one with the heart of ice. Even knowing you as I do, I was surprised when you agreed to move in with me so readily.'

'You gave me very little choice in the matter,' she reminded him. 'Waving huge debts over my head—debts, I might add, I knew nothing about until you told me.'

'And the one thing you do not like to be is short of money, is it, Nikki?' he said. 'You would do anything, including live with a man you rejected previously, for financial gain.'

Nikki knew there was no way to defend herself, for unless she told him of her reasons for marrying his stepfather, he would always believe her to be a gold-digger.

'I did what I thought was the right thing at the time,' she said. 'I'm sorry you got hurt. It wasn't my intention. I had no idea you were developing such strong feelings for me.'

'Do not play me for a fool!' he thundered. 'You knew exactly what you were doing. You led me on until you had me where you wanted me, and then you tossed me aside for the bigger prize.'

She turned away from him, her hands wrapping across her body, her emotions feeling as if they were unravelling. 'Please don't make me hate you any more than I already do, Massimo.'

'You are going to hate me even more,' he said. 'For I have uncovered even more of your late husband's debts for which I will want to be paid.'

Her knuckles whitened as she held herself even tighter. 'How much did he owe in total?' she asked.

'More than you would want to know,' he said. 'It seems my stepfather lost more than his flare for business in the months before he died. He lost his lucky streak as well.'

Nikki turned around to face him. 'He was very ill,' she said. 'I nursed him through each agonising second of it. I know he liked to gamble from time to time, but I saw no indication it was getting out of control.'

'Perhaps you should have kept a closer eye on the accounts,' he said. 'But then as I said this morning, I suppose you were far happier with the "he earns it you spend it" arrangement of a marriage such as yours.'

She glared at him resentfully. 'You know nothing of my marriage to your stepfather—nothing.'

'I know it cannot have been very fulfilling for you over the past few months.' His smouldering gaze ran over her suggestively. 'You have the look of a woman crying out for sensual release.'

Nikki clenched her teeth. 'Of course someone like you *would* think that,' she said. 'All you ever think about is satisfying your disgusting animal urges.'

He closed the small distance between them, his pelvis brushing against hers as his hand reached for a long strand of her hair. 'You have the very same urges, Nikki,' he said softly, bringing her hair up to his nose, his nostrils flaring as he breathed in the flowery fragrance clinging to the silky strands. 'I can see them, I can feel them, and I can smell them on your skin.'

Nikki held her breath as his dark eyes held hers, the tether of her hair keeping her so close to him she could see the widening of his pupils in desire.

'What do you say, *cara*?' He kissed the corner of her mouth before continuing, inching closer and closer to her already tingling lips. 'Why don't we get these disgusting animal urges out of the way, mmm?'

Nikki felt her heart going like a jackhammer in her chest. 'I don't like your reasons for wanting to renew our relationship.'

'By that I take it you mean revenge?'

Her tongue came out to moisten her lips. 'Yes,' she said. 'You hate me.'

'I do not love you as I did five years ago, but I do desire you.'

'Gee, thanks.'

He frowned at her dry comment. 'What did you expect me to say—that I have never stopped loving you?'

'No, of course not,' she said, biting her lip again.

'But you would prefer it if I had some sort of feeling for you other than lust?'

She frowned in distaste. 'Lust is such a horrible word.'

'I cannot wrap up in romantic wrapping what I feel for you now,' he said. 'But who knows? We might over time restore some of what we had that week five years ago.'

'You will never forgive me for marrying your stepfather, no matter what my motives were at the time,' she said.

'I do not wish to speak of him again.'

'He wasn't a bad person, Massimo.'

'I do not want him to be the third person in our relationship,' he stated implacably. 'I understand you loved him, but I would prefer it if you would refrain from reminding me of it at every opportunity.'

She pulled herself out of his hold, this time successfully. 'We do *not* have a relationship.'

'Not yet,' he said. 'But I have a feeling you will soon change your mind.'

She opened her mouth to deny it, but he pressed her lips together with the tip of his finger. 'Hush, *cara*,' he said with a mocking smile. 'I do not want you to have too many words to eat later, for there will be no room for our dinner, eh?'

She slapped his hand away from her mouth. 'There's not going to be any dinner—or at least none cooked by me,' she said.

Massimo watched her stalk out, her blonde hair swinging in fury, the door snipping shut behind her.

He blew out a breath and looked down at the little cat who was blinking up at him with green eyes full of reproach, as she waited for the door to be opened again so she too could leave.

'I suppose it is to be expected that you would stick up for her, Pia,' he said wryly. 'For you are both female and both not very good at following orders.'

Pia gave him one last look over her shoulder and stalked out, her long, black tail twitching in disapproval.

CHAPTER NINE

Nikki had hoped to avoid another confrontation with Massimo, so deliberately delayed coming downstairs the next morning but he had clearly anticipated her actions, for she found him in the kitchen lingering over his coffee and reading the morning paper.

He looked up when she came in and informed her, 'I have made the travel arrangements for tomorrow. We leave at 6 a.m. in my private jet, landing in Palermo, where I have a villa.'

'How wonderful it must be to have so much money to throw around,' she said with a toss of her head as she reached for the orange juice. 'I don't see why we couldn't have taken a commercial flight just like everyone else. There is such a thing as business class, you know.'

'I have worked hard for what I have, and see no problem in making such long and arduous journeys as comfortable as I can,' he returned. 'However if your conscience is troubling you I can book you on a commercial carrier on a business-class fare—or perhaps you would prefer economy? I will of course continue with the arrangements I have made for myself.'

Her top lip turned up in disdain. 'Of course.'

He drew in a harsh breath and placed his half-finished coffee on the bench with a sharp crack. 'I am losing my patience with you, Nikki,' he said. 'I was thinking of your comfort as well as my own.'

'I just bet you were,' she tossed back.

'What is that supposed to mean?'

'I want my own room at your villa,' she said with a determined set to her chin. 'In fact, I want my own room wherever we stay.'

'I am afraid that will not be possible,' he said.

'Why?' She sent him a scornful glance. 'Is your billionaire villa too small or something?'

'No,' he said. 'There are numerous rooms, but each of them is serviced by my attentive housekeeper.'

Nikki felt a little alarm bell ringing inside her head. 'So?'

'So, *la mia piccola padrona*,' he drawled. 'We will have to share a room for the sake of appearances.'

Her eyes flared with anger. 'I will do no such thing!'

'You are travelling as my intimate companion, Nikki,' he said. 'My staff members are used to me having my latest lover share my room, and will expect you to do so, as well. Besides, my ex-lover will suspect something if things do not appear normal between us.'

Nikki drew her brows together. 'Your ex-mistress lives in Sicily?'

'Yes.'

'Then she must have incredibly long-range vision, for I thought the whole reason I was acting as your mistress here in Melbourne was for her benefit,' she said with a sharp edge to her voice.

'It is.'

'How does that work?' she asked, her eyes still narrowed in suspicion.

'Sabrina Gambari has family in Australia,' he said. 'I wanted them to hear of our relationship, so when we arrive in Palermo there will not be a problem.'

She folded her arms crossly. 'You hope.'

'I do not anticipate any trouble now that the news has gotten out about our involvement,' he said. 'Her family had hopes of a marriage between us, but hearing you and I are together will hopefully defuse such dreams.'

'You weren't interested in marrying her?'

'No,' he said. 'After what happened to my father I do not think it is wise to commit yourself to one woman, who can then turn the tables on you so heartlessly.'

'I suppose that is meant to be a dig at me, as well,' she said with a resentful frown.

He gave her a look which said 'if the shoe fits'. 'I will see you tonight,' he said. 'Do not bother to cook. We will dine out instead.'

'I don't want to go out,' she said. 'I need to pack.'

'You have the rest of today to pack, *cara*,' he said. 'You are a lady of leisure now, are you not?'

'For how long?' she asked with a glowering look.

'Until the debt you owe me is cleared.'

'How do I know you're not going to string this out indefinitely?' she asked. 'You keep finding debts to hang over my head.'

He came over to where she was standing and lifted her chin, making her eyes meet his. 'To hasten things up, you can make the first installment any time you like, Nikki.'

Her grey-blue eyes flashed at him. 'I'm not going to lower myself in such a way.'

His eyes turned black as they burned into hers. 'If I had

time I would make you eat every one of those foolish words. You are indeed very lucky I have a meeting to attend, otherwise you would be spreadeagled on that table by now, with me proving how much you want me.'

Nikki felt her stomach cave in at the sexy promise of his statement. Her heart fluttered and stopped, fluttered and got going again, but in an out-of-time rhythm. She stood transfixed as his head came down, his mouth swooping to capture hers in a bruising kiss that was brief, but no less devastating.

He stepped back from her, picked up his keys and briefcase, and, with a searing look that she felt at the very base of her spine, he left.

Nikki caught a cab to Rosedale House, spending the afternoon with her younger brother, pushing him around the gardens as she told him of her forthcoming trip.

'I won't be able to see you for a couple of weeks,' she said as she sat on one of the benches near a bed of colourful azaleas. 'I know it's very short notice, but I'll be back before you know it.'

Jayden blinked at her vacuously, and Nikki squeezed his hand as she fought back tears. 'I'm so sorry, Jayden,' she choked out. 'If I could turn back the clock you know I would do it. I should be sitting in that chair, not you. I can never forgive myself for moving out of the way. I saw him coming for me, and I didn't realise you would take the brunt of his violence instead...'

She clasped Jayden's hand in both of her hands, tears streaming down her face. 'I love you, Jayden,' she said. 'I know you can't really understand a word I say, but I love you with everything that is in me. I will fight for you with my last breath, I swear I will.'

Nikki spent the remainder of the afternoon with some of the other residents, reading to them and helping with the drinks and snacks that came around at tea time. The staff knew her as plain Nicola Burnside, and with her blonde hair scraped back in a ponytail, no make-up, and wearing her oldest jeans and sweater, no one had ever questioned her identity. Nikki was amazed she had been able to get away with it for so long, but it suited her to keep her public life totally separate. Joseph had never questioned her outings, assuming she was visiting friends or shopping, and she had never once enlightened him.

But occasionally, particularly in those last heart-wrenching weeks as he had slowly and agonisingly faded, she had felt tempted to reveal her private pain. She had wanted to thank him for what he had done in providing such wonderful care for her brother, but every time she'd tried to form the words she just hadn't been able do it.

Her past was in the past and talking about it wouldn't change Jayden's life one iota. His future had been stolen, and it was up to her to give him what comfort she could, no matter what the cost.

But as she left to make her way back to Massimo's house, Nikki had to concede that perhaps the price was going to be a whole lot higher than she had ever imagined.

Massimo found her sitting in the lounge with the cat on her lap when he came in from work. 'I called you several times today,' he said. 'Where were you?'

'I went shopping,' she said, almost but not quite meeting his eyes.

'What did you buy?'

'Nothing.'

He raised his brows. 'Nothing at all?'

The cat leapt off her lap as Nikki got to her feet. 'You did say I wasn't to be chained to the house, if you remember,' she said. 'Or would you prefer me to sign in and out?'

'I would prefer to know where you are,' he said.

'Why?' she asked. 'So you can monitor my movements like a prison guard?'

'Not at all,' he responded evenly. 'I am merely thinking of your safety.'

'I hardly think shopping is a life-threatening pastime,' she said.

'Perhaps not, but I would still prefer you to use Ricardo for transport rather than use public transport.'

'I can look after myself.'

His dark gaze wandered over her in an assessing manner. 'You are far too thin, Nikki. You look as if a breeze could knock you over. You would not stand a chance if someone was intent on snatching your purse or jewellery.'

'I'm a model, or at least I was until a couple of days ago,' she shot back. 'I'm supposed to be slim.'

'You are unhappy about me severing your contract?'

Nikki was, but not for the reasons he thought. 'I would have liked to discuss it first,' she said.

'We can discuss it over dinner. I also wish to discuss the design contract with you,' he said. 'Are you ready to leave?'

She gave him a heated glare without responding, and, snatching up her bag, accompanied him out to the car where Ricardo was waiting to take them to the restaurant.

The table they were led to a short time later was set well back from the others in a private corner, the lighting low and intimate.

Nikki buried her head in the menu rather than meet Massimo's gaze, her senses on high alert with him sitting so close. She knew she had only to stretch out her legs to come into contact with him, the sudden temptation to do so almost overwhelming.

'Relax, Nikki,' he said as she wriggled on her chair. 'I do not want people to think you would rather be anywhere but here.'

'I *would* rather be anywhere but here,' she said with a little scowl.

'So would I,' he returned with a slow, sexy smile. 'In bed, for instance, with your legs wrapped around mine.'

'I didn't mean that!' she said, and buried her head back in the menu again.

He chuckled softly. 'You are like an open book, Nikki. I can see you are doing your best to string out the period of time before we reconsummate our relationship, but it is getting harder and harder, is it not?'

'I'm doing no such thing.'

'Are you hoping by making me wait it will drive the price up even more?' he asked. 'If you are, it is working. I am hard just sitting here looking at you.'

She sent him a fulminating look, her cheeks flaring with heat. 'You really are contemptible. I hadn't realised until now how much so.'

'You want the whole deal, do you not?' he asked with an indolent expression. 'Being a mistress has never interested you. You want marriage, but I am equally determined not to offer it to you.'

She tossed her blonde hair back over her shoulders. 'I wouldn't accept it if you did.'

His dark eyes hardened. 'Do not play games with me, *cara*,' he warned. 'You will not win this time around. You and I have a past score to settle and we will settle it in my bed.'

Nikki glared at him. 'How many times do I have to tell you I don't want to sleep with you?'

'I would find it easier to believe you if your body was sending me the same message, but it is not,' he said. 'You *do* want to sleep with me, and sleep with me you will, as of tonight.'

She disguised her rush of panic with a voice dripping with disdain. 'You're going to have to try a whole lot harder if you want me to shove my memories of Joseph aside to make room for you.'

His anger crackled in the air separating them. Nikki knew she was being reckless, goading him, but she couldn't seem to stop it. It wasn't as if he could think any less of her than he already did.

'I swear to God, Nikki, that I will make you forget that man,' he ground out. 'I will have my name on your lips, not his. Do you hear me?'

She set her mouth, her eyes firing sparks of defiance at him. 'You think.'

He leaned forward, his voice a low, primal growl. 'Before this night is over I will have you sobbing my name like you did that night five years ago. Your body will throb and hum with the release I know you crave from me, and only me.'

Nikki opened her mouth to fling a retort his way when the waiter appeared to take their order. She schooled her features into a bland indifference and ordered the first thing she saw, knowing she wouldn't be able to get a single mouthful past the lump of pain tightening her throat.

She sat in a stony silence for the rest of the meal, refusing to engage in the attempts at conversation Massimo occasionally made for the sake of appearances. She could see the way his anger was rising with each of the chilly looks she sent his way; his lips turned white at one point, his eyes warning her there would be hell to pay for her very public insurgence.

She gave her head a toss and drank another glass of wine, her head swimming slightly from the unfamiliar amount of alcohol.

'You are going to regret that in the morning,' Massimo said as she put her glass back down.

'I don't care,' she said.

He tossed his napkin down and got to his feet. 'We are leaving,' he said implacably.

She gave him a belligerent look. 'I'm not ready to leave.'

His dark eyes warred with hers and won. She lowered her gaze and reached for her bag, following him out of the restaurant with a sinking feeling in the pit of her stomach.

He didn't speak for the entire journey, and Nikki knew she had pushed him too far. The swish of the tyres on the wet roads filled the brittle silence, the back and forth motion of the windscreen wipers making her eyes water as she tried to focus on them rather than the rigid figure beside her.

The car purred into the huge garage like a panther returning to its den, and Nikki felt her stomach tighten another excruciating notch as the engine gave a low growl before going silent.

She waited as Massimo came around to open her door, her eyes avoiding his as she exited the car.

The click-clack of her heels was almost unbearably loud in the cold, still night air. Even the key turning in the lock sounded like a gun shot, her tautly stretched nerves making her inwardly jump.

He put a hand in the small of her back and led her indoors, turning to face her once the door had closed behind them.

'I am not going to give you the satisfaction of acting like the unfeeling brute you think I am by responding to your very deliberate attempts to make me lose my temper,' he said. 'That is what that routine in the restaurant was all about, was it not?'

She couldn't hold his gaze. 'I'm sorry,' she whispered.

'Nikki, Nikki, Nikki,' he said, and drew her towards him with arms so gentle she felt tears well at the backs of her eyes. 'You make me so angry, I want to shake you, but lucky for you I am not a violent man.'

She burrowed closer, breathing in the male scent of him, her arms going around his waist almost of their own accord.

'What am I going to do with you, *cara*?' he asked.

She pressed back to look up at him, her bottom lip trembling ever so slightly. 'I don't want you to hate me, Massimo,' she said. 'I couldn't bear to make love with a man who hates me.'

He held her gaze for a lengthy moment. 'I cannot pretend feelings I no longer have,' he said. 'You surely understand that?'

Her gaze fell away from his. 'Yes, I do understand that.'

He lifted her chin. 'But it makes you sad, mmm?'

'A lot of things make me sad, Massimo,' she said softly. 'A lot of things.'

He brushed a loose strand of blonde hair back from her face, tucking it gently behind her ear. 'I am in two minds over you, *cara*,' he confessed wryly. 'One tells me to let you go, and the other tells me to have my fill of you. Which one should I listen to, I wonder?'

Nikki held her breath as his mouth came closer, the brush of his breath against her lips kick-starting her pulse. She swallowed as his tongue glided across the surface of her lips, the tantalising movement sending sparks of heat right to her toes and back.

She told herself to move out of his embrace before it was too late, but it was as if her body and brain were no longer connected. Passion had shorted the system until all she could do was move closer and closer, her mouth opening under the increasing pressure of his, her arms going from around his waist to his neck in blissful abandon, her fingers delving into the black silk of his hair.

He made a sound of pleasure deep in his throat as her tongue slid forward to meet his, the intimate, moist coupling one of fevered urgency as if all hope of control had finally slipped out of his grasp.

His hands were on her breasts, his palms moulding her, caressing her through her clothes, until she was desperate to feel his skin on hers.

When he lifted her in his arms she made a tiny token sound of protest, but his mouth came back to hers to smother it.

'No, *cara mia*,' he said as he carried her towards the sweeping staircase. 'There is no turning back now. It is our time again at last.'

Nikki shivered in pleasure as Massimo's hands dealt with her clothes, his mouth kissing every bare inch of flesh as he uncovered it. He removed her bra, his hands skating over her full breasts, his eyes feasting on her until she felt her belly quivering with anticipation. He bent his mouth to her right breast and suckled on it, drawing the aching nipple into his mouth, his tongue rolling over and over it until her back came off the bed. Her left breast was subjected to the same exquisite torture, the pull of his hot mouth triggering a moist response deep in her feminine core.

He slid the zip of her skirt down and peeled away her tights, leaving her with nothing but her tiny knickers. She felt the scorch of his gaze as he cupped her tender mound, his fingers so close to where she pulsed for him she was sure he would be able to feel the drumbeat of desire against his palm.

She sucked in a sharp breath as he tugged the black lace away. 'You're not undressed,' she said raggedly.

'I know,' he said, lowering his head to the tiny indentation of her belly button, his breath whispering over her abdomen. 'I have other things on my mind right now.'

Nikki clutched at the sheets with clawing fingers as his mouth moved lower, his tongue leaving a glistening trail of fire all the way down to the tiny landing-strip of closely cropped curls that shielded her femininity. She gasped as his tongue separated her, the first rasping stroke against her making every single fine hair on her body stand to attention.

'You still taste of salt and sugar,' he said, moving back up her body with deliberate slowness, each movement of his lips sending another current of fire through her system.

Nikki wanted to taste and feel him, too. She tugged at his shirt, pulling it out of his trousers and tossing it over the edge of the bed. She pressed hot, little moist kisses to the naked skin of his chest, her fingers lacing through the sprinkling of dark hair, delighting in the feel of his arrant masculinity.

She undid his belt and slid it out of his trousers, and sent it in the same direction as his shirt, her fingers going to the fastening at his waist before releasing his zip. His thickness tented his black underwear and she pulled it out of the way to access him.

He groaned as she bent her head to him. *'Eiaculò troppo velocemente.'*

She ran her tongue down the silky shaft before asking, 'What does that mean?'

He flinched as she did it again. 'I will come too quickly,' he said, groaning as she bent her head again.

She opened her mouth over him, tasting his musky saltiness, feeling the glide of his satin-covered steel.

'Il mio dio,' he groaned again, his fingers digging into her hair. 'Stop now.'

'I don't want to stop.'

He swore and rolled her off him, pinning her beneath him, his body surging forward, parting her in one rough thrust. Her slick moistness welcomed him, her tight muscles clenching him possessively, her hips rising and falling as she followed his frantic rhythm. Her breath came in fevered gasps as the pace increased, beads of perspiration peppering her skin where the heat of his rocked against her.

She was so close, but not quite there when he began to massage her intimately, his long fingers playing her like an instrument until she was suddenly soaring. She hit the highest note of pleasure, the taut strings of her senses reverberating with wave after wave of rapture.

She felt his body tense momentarily above hers, the precursor to his freefall into oblivion. She held him as he shuddered through it, spilling himself into the warm cocoon of her body, until he collapsed against her, his hurried breath feathering the side of her neck where his face was pressed.

She stroked her hands over his back with long, massaging movements, rediscovering his muscular contours, her body still tingling from the heat and driving force of his.

She felt the slow trickle of his essence between her legs, and suddenly stiffened. 'Oh, no…'

Massimo propped himself on his elbows and looked down at her, his expression shadowed with concern. 'I have hurt you?'

'No, it's just that I… I mean, we didn't use protection. I'm not on the pill.'

He got off the bed in one lithe movement, the anger coming off him in rippling waves even though his voice was deceptively calm. 'Do you not think it might have been appropriate to tell me that a few minutes ago?' he asked.

Stung by the tone of accusation in his voice, she shot back defensively, 'You didn't exactly give me much time.'

His mouth tightened to a thin white line. 'So you are blaming *me*?'

She met his glittering glare with an equanimity she was nowhere near feeling. 'If you were so concerned you should have protected yourself, or is it a habit of yours to have unsafe sex?'

'No, it is not,' he said, his eyes narrowing slightly as he added, 'But then perhaps you planned it this way.'

Nikki refused to respond; besides, she could almost guess where his mind was heading.

'It is indeed an old trick, but a good one,' he said. 'If you were to fall pregnant it would give you a much bigger bargaining tool, would it not?'

'I'd rather die than have any child of yours,' she said with a fiery glare.

His mouth tightened even further. 'I thought I told you I will not have you speak to me so insultingly.'

She pulled her shoulders back in defiance. 'I will speak to you any way I like,' she said. 'You paid me to be your pretend mistress, not your subservient slave.'

There was a thick, pulsating silence.

'Thank you for reminding me,' he said coolly and reached for his trousers on the floor.

Nikki's mouth went dry as she watched him take out his wallet from the back pocket, his fingers unfolding it to take out a wad of cash.

'That should just about cover it,' he said, and dropped the cash on the bed.

She opened and closed her mouth, caught between a fury so intense and despair so deep she couldn't get a single word out. She stood in a helpless silence as he stepped back into his trousers, socks and shoes before reaching for a fresh shirt from the walk-in wardrobe, tucking it in as he came back to where she was standing.

'I am going out,' he announced.

'Do you think I care?' she bit out.

'Probably not, but I thought I should tell you all the same,' he said. 'I wouldn't want you to wait up for me unnecessarily.'

'Isn't that what a good little obedient mistress is supposed to do?' she asked with a curl of her lip.

His eyes held hers in a battle of wills that saw her drop her gaze first. She turned away, holding her arms close to her body, pain filling her chest until she could scarcely breathe.

'It doesn't have to be this way between us, Nikki,' he said after another long silence.

She clamped her bottom lip between her teeth, determined not to respond. But in a matter of seconds she heard the rustle of his clothes as he moved across the room, and the soft click of the door as it shut behind him.

CHAPTER TEN

THE flight to Palermo was long and tiring, in spite of the luxury of travelling in a private jet with attentive staff seeing to their every need. More in an effort to avoid conversation with Massimo, Nikki pleaded tiredness and lay down in the sleeping compartment, and, although she barely slept for more than a few minutes at a stretch, she was relieved he didn't join her. What his flight crew made of it she was beyond caring. She was still nursing her hurt from the night before. If only he knew how deeply he had insulted her. It had been so tempting to defend herself but she knew he would never have believed her. After all, she had married his stepfather, and Joseph had obviously led Massimo to believe their marriage was a real one.

Yet another member of staff met them at the airport and drove them to the villa overlooking the chief seaport of Sicily. The salty tang of the sea was heavy in the air, the bright summer sunshine a stark contrast to the capricious winter of Melbourne. Nikki breathed it in, her skin feeling as if the top layers were swelling in response to the delicious warmth of the sun.

A housekeeper with the name of Carine showed her to the master suite once they had made their way indoors. 'Signore

Androletti has instructed me to unpack for you,' she said. 'Do you need anything pressed for dinner this evening?'

'No, thank you,' Nikki said with a small smile. 'I'm used to seeing to things myself.'

The young woman looked confused. 'But you are a model, no?'

'I haven't modelled for months. I'm not used to being waited on any more; I prefer to look after myself,' Nikki said. 'Please don't trouble yourself. I've brought easy-care clothes in any case.'

'You are very different from Signore Androletti's usual partners,' the young woman observed.

Nikki couldn't resist asking, 'In what way?'

Carine made a little moue with her mouth. 'That last one, she was nothing but trouble, always wanting things at all hours of the day and night. I had to run errands for her all the time until my legs hurt.'

'I promise not to do that to you,' Nikki said with another friendly smile. 'Believe me, I'm very low-maintenance.'

Carine tilted her head as she looked at her. 'You are very beautiful, much more beautiful than her, although she too is blonde and tall—although if you ask me her hair colour comes out of a bottle.'

So, he has a thing for tall blondes, Nikki thought with a sharp little pang of jealousy. 'I'll try not to be too much trouble for you,' she said.

'I do not think you could ever be anything but good for Signore Androletti,' Carine said with passionate emphasis. 'He used to be such an easygoing man, but over the last few years he has…how you say in English…a chip on his shoulder?'

'Um…yes,' Nikki said, her face feeling a little hot. 'That's right, a chip on his shoulder.'

'See? I am learning good English from you already!' Carine said excitedly. 'Signorina Gambari would not even speak to me in Italian, let alone English. But you are not like that, I can tell. You are a nice lady. You must have had good upbringing, yes?'

'Er, yes,' Nikki lied. 'Very good.'

'I knew it,' Carine said as she straightened the bed covering with a proud little stroke of her hand. 'A good background is *importante*, no?'

'Very,' Nikki agreed.

'If you want me to do anything for you just call me,' Carine said.

'I will. Thank you.'

Carine smiled. 'I hope he asks *you* to be his wife,' she said. 'It is what he needs, a wife and a couple of *bambinos* to make him settle down. He has been playing for too hard and for too long.'

'Carine, would you please leave us?' Massimo's voice spoke from the door.

'*Sì, signore.*' Carine bowed her head subserviently and scuttled away.

Nikki turned on him in anger. 'There was no need to dismiss her so coldly,' she said. 'She is fond of you, who knows why, but she is.'

'I do not like to be the subject of my staff's speculations,' he said. 'Carine has a habit of speaking out of turn.'

'She is very young,' Nikki said in the young woman's defence. 'She is eager to please and shouldn't be repri-manded for it.'

He raised a brow at her. 'You are very good at this, are you not?' he asked. 'Worming your way into everyone's affections.'

'Except yours, of course,' she said with an element of bitterness.

'I have made my feelings towards you very clear.'

She sent him a churlish look. 'Yes, that's true. More than clear.'

He came to where she was standing, his eyes holding hers. 'You are still angry with me, eh, Nikki?' he asked.

'Yes, I am,' she said, glaring at him. 'What you did was unforgiveable.'

'That was our agreement, was it not? That you would be my mistress for a price.'

'I didn't sleep with you for money, and you know it,' she said.

'Then why did you sleep with me?'

Good question, Nikki thought. She lowered her gaze from the intensity of his. 'I didn't really intend for things to go that far,' she said. 'I thought I'd be able to stop at any point…'

'But you could not?'

His tone brought her eyes back to his. 'No,' she said, releasing a small sigh. 'I could not.'

He touched her cheek with the end of one long finger in a brushlike motion. 'Nor could I, *cara,*' he confessed. 'You are like a fever in my blood. I can feel you running like a hot river underneath my skin every time I look at you. No one else has ever made me feel this way.'

'But you don't love me.'

His mouth twisted with a hint of cynicism. 'You sound so genuinely disappointed, Nikki. I am almost tempted to believe you are developing feelings for me.'

'Massimo, I...'

He pressed her mouth closed with the pad of his thumb. 'No, *cara*,' he said. 'I do not want to hear empty words and phrases from you. We have a relationship built on mutual need, let's keep it at that. We will have our affair and at the end of it you will be free from the debts your late husband left you with. That is a bargain, is it not?'

It is a sure path to heartbreak, Nikki thought as his mouth came down to cover hers. Her lips swelled under the intoxicating pressure of his kiss, the first touch of his tongue against hers sending sparks of desire up and down her legs and the length of her spine. Her whole body responded in a rush of heady feeling, her skin tightening all over at the thought of his hands touching her the way he had touched her before. She pushed herself closer, her breasts crushed against his chest as her mouth fed hungrily off his, her soft whimpers of need fuelling him to deepen the kiss to a mind-blowing assault on her senses.

His hands moved to cup the gentle weight of her breasts, his thumbs rolling over the already tight buds of her nipples, triggering another whimper of pleasure from her throat.

'You want me just as much as I want you,' he said, momentarily lifting his mouth from hers. 'I feel it in your body; the pressure of longing is uncontrollable.'

Nikki didn't bother denying it. She pulled his head back down to her mouth and pushed her tongue between his lips to find his, curling around it with seductive little movements that made him growl as he began to deal with the barrier of her clothes.

Her lightweight skirt and top were soon dispensed with, his clothes, under the frantic and fumbling movement of her hands, joining them on the floor at their feet.

She caressed him through the fabric of his underwear, teasing him with each stroke of her hand until he wrenched the fabric away with a muttered curse of frustration.

Her fingers encircled him boldly, the satin-covered steel of his body making her shiver in anticipation at its alluring control over her. She felt the thrumming pulse of her body between her legs until it became an intense ache for assuagement. She rubbed against him unashamedly, her lower body on fire for the heat and power of his.

He wrenched his mouth away from hers long enough to growl, 'You are making me crazy for you. I am not going to be able to hold back.'

Nikki didn't want him to hold back, she wanted him to be as desperate and needy as she was. She pushed herself closer, her fingers digging into the taut flesh of his buttocks to bring him to her needy core.

He pushed her away to remove her bra before his hands went to her tiny lacy briefs. She felt the delicate tickle of lace being pulled down over her thighs as he knelt before her, and then the hot breeze of his breath as he cradled her hips in his hands to explore her melting form. Each and every hair on her head rose at the first flicker of his tongue against her, and her back arched in delight as he tasted her. Her fingers dug into his scalp at that first, sexy rasp of his tongue against the swollen pearl of her need, the sensations building to fever pitch until she felt every nerve tightening to snapping point.

The first wave of release hit her, closely followed by a second and third, each more devastating than the previous one. Her whole body shook and shuddered with the aftershocks, her legs still trembling as he straightened.

Nikki found it hard to look into his eyes in case he saw the truth of her feelings shining back at him. She concentrated on the fine sheen of perspiration on his chest, pressing her mouth to each of his dark-brown nipples, running her tongue over each one in turn before trailing a pathway to his belly button. She felt his body jerk in response as she began to go lower, his hands burying into her hair, a deep groan issuing from his throat at the first brush of her lips against his turgid length.

She knew he was close to losing control, she could feel the hair-trigger tension in his body, his deeply in-drawn breath signalling he was moving beyond the point of no return. She opened her mouth over him and drew on him again and again, stronger and stronger, until she felt him explode with a hot burst of male power that made her stomach hollow out in reaction as she tasted him fully for the first time.

The raw intimacy of what she had just done surprised her no less than it surprised him.

'You have certainly learnt a few tricks from my stepfather,' he said with a flicker of something she didn't care for in his eyes. 'And here I was thinking perhaps he had been boasting about your sexual expertise.'

'He *was* boasting,' she said emphatically. 'I never slept with your stepfather.'

His mouth became white-tipped with anger. 'Do not insult my intelligence with such a pathetic lie.'

'It's the truth,' she said. 'He couldn't, for one thing, and I wouldn't have even if he had been able to perform.'

He scooped up her clothing from the floor and thrust it at her. 'Get dressed.' He clipped the words out savagely. 'I do not want to listen to any more of this nonsense.'

'It's not nonsense!' Nikki insisted as he turned away to retrieve his own clothes. 'I didn't have a sexual relationship with Joseph. He had prostate cancer. He didn't want anyone to know how he'd become impotent after the radical surgical procedure had been performed. It devastated him, as indeed it would any man.'

He turned around to face her, his expression communicating his disbelief. 'So you felt sorry for him and married him, did you, Nikki? For money, right? Lots and lots of money, if I recall.'

Nikki couldn't bear to see the contempt in his glittering gaze and lowered her eyes. 'I told you my reasons for marrying your stepfather,' she said.

'Yes, you did, and you are with me for the very same reason, are you not?' he asked. 'Money motivates you to do almost anything, right, Nikki?'

She forced her gaze back to his. 'I am not ashamed of marrying your stepfather. He helped me when I needed help and treated me with nothing but respect.'

His eyes hardened as they pierced hers. 'You are not ashamed because you are without shame,' he said. 'You use people to get what you want and suffer no remorse about it.'

'That is more accurately a description of you, not me,' she threw back. 'You have exploited me in the most despicable way, treating me like a whore, when in the last five years I have never slept with anyone but you.'

His bark of mocking laughter made Nikki feel sick with anguish. 'Nice try, Nikki,' he said. 'You almost had me there. It is certainly a cute story, but like all fairy tales totally outside the realm of reality.'

'There's no way I can make you believe me, I know that,' she said. 'You are too bitter and angry for the truth to get a foothold. But what if you're wrong about me, Massimo?'

His dark gaze stripped her. 'I know what you are, Nikki. You are a social climber. You have lied to me from the very beginning, just as you lie to everyone you meet—even my housekeeper Carine just a short time ago.'

Nikki felt a tiny tremor of alarm rumble through her at his tone.

'You see, Nikki,' he went on. 'I have made some interesting observations about you.'

She swallowed back her rising panic. She told herself there was no way he could know about her past. No one knew. She had changed her name when she'd moved from Perth. The police had assured her the witness-protection scheme was secure.

'Are you not going to ask me what I have observed about you?' he asked.

Nikki swept her tongue across her lips. 'No, but I'm sure you're going to tell me anyway.'

His eyes held hers in silence for several agonising seconds.

'I would not have thought anything of it, but I got to wondering why your family was not at my stepfather's funeral. Every time you spoke of them in the past you painted a picture of familial bliss. Where were they when you needed them most, Nikki?'

She lowered her gaze. 'We had a falling out a…a couple of years ago…'

'What was it about?'

'Um…' *Oh God!* Why couldn't she think of something convincing under the pressure of his dark, probing gaze?

'What are you trying to hide from me, Nikki?' he asked into the pulsing silence.

She forced herself to hold his penetrating look. 'I came

from an unhappy home,' she said, trying to control the wobble in her voice. 'I know it's not exactly unusual in this day
and age, but I was always ashamed of where we lived. There
wasn't a lot of money and we moved a lot.'

Massimo frowned. 'Why did you feel it necessary to hide
that from me five years ago?'

'I hate talking about my family life,' she said, her bottom
lip trembling ever so slightly he almost missed it.

She sighed and continued in the same deadened tone, 'I
spent my childhood dreaming of a perfect home, with a
mother and father who loved each other and their children.
My brother and I were an inconvenience. My father made it
quite clear we were to be seen and not heard. My mother spent
most of her life trying to keep us quiet in case we upset him.
That's pretty much it. I know it probably seems a bit lame to
you, but I got tired of making excuses for my parents. They
should never have had children.'

'Do you still see them?'

She shook her head. 'My mother is dead and I have since
severed all contact with my father.'

'What about your brother?'

She hesitated, her eyes moving away from his again. 'My
brother and I are not as close as we once were,' she said. 'We
see each other occasionally, but we don't really communicate
all that much.'

Massimo found it intriguing to hear of her past. Although
he could not forgive her for how she had exploited him, it certainly explained a lot about her greed for money and security.
She had married his stepfather for money and to launch her
career as a model, a career which he could see now had been
as far removed from her impoverished background as any

could be. She had worn the best of clothes and jewellery, eaten at the finest restaurants, drunk the most expensive wine, attended red-carpet movie premieres and stage shows with other celebrities as if she had been born to it.

But finding out all this now didn't mean he was going to allow her another chance to get her hooks into him. He would have his affair with her and call an end to it when it suited him. For, he reasoned, if she had cared anything for him five years ago she would have trusted him with the truth of her past. He had told her of his pain over the death of his father, and yet she had not once let on that her life had been anything but perfect.

He wasn't sure what to make of her claim that she had not slept with Joseph Ferliani. The reasons she'd given were certainly feasible, but he had been a victim of her deceit before, and wasn't keen on repeating the mistake of trusting that wide-eyed innocence.

However, he would have had to be blind not to recognise it had been difficult for her to open up to him now. Her whole demeanour suggested her confession had been nothing short of emotional torture. Her eyes looked wounded, and her face pale and pinched.

'Thank you for telling me,' he said into the silence. 'I am sorry if it caused you unnecessary pain.'

'I am used to it, believe me,' she said. 'But I would prefer it if we didn't have to speak of it again.'

'If that is what you want then the subject will be closed as of now.'

She looked down at her clothes still clutched against her chest. 'I guess I should get dressed.'

'No,' he said, removing them from her grasp. 'Not yet.'

Nikki looked up into his dark brown eyes and felt herself melt with longing. His hands went to her waist, their warmth seeping into her skin as he brought her closer to his hardening body. She closed her eyes as his mouth joined hers, her whole body sighing in pleasure as his tongue flicked against hers.

Nikki felt the subtle change in his kiss and touch, as if the anger of how she had treated him had gradually faded to be replaced by a longing that had nothing to do with revenge.

Her heart bursting with long-held-back feelings, she kissed him back with fervent passion, her arms looping around his neck, her pelvis pressed against the burning heat of his.

He scooped her up and brought her down to the bed, his weight coming down over her, pinning her beneath him. She felt him reach across to retrieve a condom from the bedside table drawer, deftly applying it before moving between her legs to possess her with a tenderness she found totally enthralling.

He gradually increased his pace, pulling her along with him in an exhilarating climb to the highest pinnacle of human pleasure. She was tipped over the edge by the brush strokes of his fingers playing her like a delicately tuned instrument. He joined her moments later with a deep groan of release that reverberated throughout his body. She felt and heard his sigh, and, still intimately joined, she nestled closer, her eyelashes drifting down in contentment.

Massimo listened to the gentle sound of her breathing, his hands idly playing with her hair where it lay in a silken pool around her head and shoulders. Her beautiful face was relaxed, her mouth softly swollen from his kisses, the mauve shadows under her eyes reminding him of his own exhaustion after the long-haul flight.

He let out a long sigh that caught on something small and prickly in his chest, and, closing his eyes, he breathed in the scent of her body, promising himself he would not stay for too long…

CHAPTER ELEVEN

NIKKI woke late the next morning to find herself alone in the big bed. She ran her fingers over the indentation in the pillow beside her, a little quiver of delight rushing through her as she thought about the passion and tenderness of the night before. Massimo had turned to her again during the early hours of the morning, his love making taking her to new heights of ecstasy.

She showered and then dressed in a light cotton sundress, with her hair scooped up in a casual knot, and made her way down to the terrace overlooking the sea where Carine had set up fresh rolls, fruit, home-made preserves and freshly brewed coffee.

'Signore Androletti will be with you shortly,' Carine said after a cheerful greeting. 'He is taking a few business calls.'

'Thank you, Carine,' she said as the housekeeper poured coffee. 'Have you worked for Signore Androletti long?'

'For three years,' Carine answered. 'I took over from my aunt who worked for the family for many years.' She handed the rolls to Nikki and added with a little look of self-consciousness, 'I guess I must not seem very ambitious compared to someone like you, working as a housekeeper instead of going after bigger and better things.'

'I'm hardly what you would call ambitious,' Nikki confessed with a slight frown. 'I haven't worked in months, and don't intend to again if I can help it.'

Carine suddenly looked past Nikki's shoulder and blushed. 'Signore Androletti,' she said. 'Your breakfast is served.'

'*Grazie*, Carine,' Massimo said. 'Could you inform Salvatore that we will be ready for the car in approximately one hour?'

Carine bowed her head. '*Sì, signore.*'

Nikki waited with bated breath as the housekeeper disappeared inside the villa. She could feel the tension coming off Massimo like a charge of electricity pulsing through the air.

'So,' he said with a brittle look as he took the chair opposite. 'You have no intention of ever returning to work. Why is that, I wonder—because you intend to land yourself another rich husband?'

Nikki moistened her lips as his dark eyes burned into hers. 'You misunderstood what I said to Carine,' she said. 'What I meant was I didn't intend to return to modelling.'

Suspicion lurked in the shadows of his gaze. 'Because I cancelled your contract?'

'No, because I am tired of it,' she said, looking away. 'I never really liked it in the first place. It was always just a job.'

'There are many women who would give anything to have had the chance for fame and fortune you have been given,' he said. 'Your face is recognisable wherever Ferliani Fashions are sold.'

Her eyes came back to his. 'The constructed image of Nikki Ferliani, yes—but it's not really me,' she said. 'Look at me, Massimo. Do I really look like the woman on the billboards?'

Massimo studied her for a moment. Her face was devoid of make-up, her hair casually arranged, some of it already escaping its clip to cascade down the sides of her heart-shaped face. He had to admit she didn't exactly look streetwise and worldly. She had a hint of fragility about her. The slightly anxious pleat of her brow, and the soft lips that had a tendency to roll together in uncertainty when she thought no one was looking, made him wonder if what she said was true—that the woman on the billboards was indeed someone else.

'You are still a very beautiful woman, *cara*,' he said. 'Even without the accoutrements of the modelling trade.'

He watched as she crumbled the roll with her fingers, her nails without colour and short as if she had nibbled at them recently.

Her grey-blue eyes met his briefly. 'Thank you.'

'Have you thought any more about my offer of a design job within the business?' he asked as he poured himself a cup of the steaming coffee.

'I'm...I'm not sure I'm the person for the job,' she said after a slight hesitation. 'I have no qualifications, and I only helped your stepfather out because he was falling behind.'

'Is there something else you would like to do?' he asked. 'You worked as a personal assistant in the business before. Would you consider a return to that?'

'I don't think it would be wise for me to get too involved,' Nikki said with a wry twist to her mouth. 'After all, I'm a temporary diversion in your life. When our affair is over, I can't imagine you wanting me underfoot at Ferliani.'

'I am not intending to keep Ferliani Fashions for very long,' he informed her. 'I have sunk considerable funds into the business, and once it recovers from the slight downturn it has experienced recently I will sell it. I already have had several enquiries. I am just waiting for the price to be driven up.'

'Ever the hard-nosed businessman,' she commented darkly.

His brows moved together over his eyes. 'You surely do not expect me to keep it indefinitely?'

Her shoulders came down on the weight of a sigh. 'No, perhaps not. It's just that your stepfather worked so hard at making it what it is.'

'You are forgetting he defrauded my father to do it,' he said. 'He used my father's hard-earned savings to fund his own dream of a fashion label.'

'I understand your bitterness,' she said. 'But both Joseph and your father are now dead. You can't change the circumstances that existed between them.'

'No, but I want justice.'

'By that I suppose you mean paying me back for rejecting you?'

He held her flinty look for several pulsing seconds. 'As far as I see it, I am being extremely generous towards you in offering to wipe out all the debt your late husband left you with, in exchange for a brief period of time as my lover.'

'The agreement was I was to be your trophy mistress,' she said, capturing her bottom lip briefly.

He paused in the process of bringing his coffee cup to his mouth. 'So the circumstances have changed a bit. It is to our mutual benefit, however, if the last two nights have been any indication.'

Nikki felt her face heating under his scrutiny. She looked down at the little mountain of crumbs she'd made with her restless fingers, her heart contracting as she wondered how long he would want her for.

Would his desire for her burn out within days, weeks or months? They had only had a week together five years ago, and, as wonderful as it had been, it didn't necessarily mean an affair for any length of time would work out now. He could tire of her within a few short weeks, which would leave her devastated. She had found it hard enough to walk away from him before—how much worse would it be this time around?

The slight rattle of his cup as he put it back on the glass-topped table brought her head back up to meet his eyes.

'I thought we could take a drive to one of the villages where the designs are manufactured,' he said. 'After there, we can do a little sightseeing for the rest of the day before stopping for dinner somewhere.'

'Fine.'

He waited another moment before adding, 'You are meant to be enjoying yourself, Nikki. You are supposed to look like a woman who is being spoilt by her attentive lover. The least you could do is smile for the benefit of my staff.'

'There is no staff around at the moment,' Nikki pointed out.

'Perhaps not, but I would still like to see you smile,' he said. 'I do not think I have seen you do so in the whole time we have been together.'

'The circumstances by which we are together are hardly the sort to bring an involuntary smile to my lips,' she remarked.

The line of his jaw stiffened as his eyes skewered hers. 'You do not give an inch, do you, Nikki? You like to twist that little knife of yours any chance you can. What do you hope to achieve by it, mmm? An apology from me, or a proposal?'

Nikki was the first to shift her gaze. 'I am not expecting much from you at all,' she said. 'You seem incapable of being anything but bitter and twisted towards me.'

'As I've told you before, if I remain bitter towards you, you have only yourself to blame,' he said. 'I do not respect a woman who marries a man she does not love for money. I can think of no single circumstance where that would ever be acceptable.'

Nikki got to her feet and, brushing the crumbs off her dress, sent him a rapier look. 'Then perhaps you're not thinking hard enough, Massimo.'

Massimo watched as she turned for the villa, her gait jerky and stilted, as if she couldn't wait to be rid of his presence. He heard the door open and close with a snap, the sound of it echoing through the villa.

A small frown began to tug at his brow as he slowly rose to his feet, his chest rising and falling on a heavy sigh as he tossed his napkin to one side and followed her indoors.

Nikki hadn't expected to enjoy the day in Massimo's company, but after they had driven to a small village about an hour and a half from Palermo the frozen silence that had accompanied them gradually thawed. As the morning progressed she could tell he was making an effort to effect some sort of truce. He involved her in all of the discussions at the factory, introducing her to the various staff members, his manner solicitous and polite throughout.

Nikki fingered the beautiful fabrics she was handed with reverence, smiling from time to time when one of the seamstresses showed her a clever invisible zip, or the delicate stitching that was a signature of a Ferliani design.

She got a particular thrill out of seeing the first of her own designs being made, the soft fall of fabric as one of the girls held it up for her inspection bringing a tiny lump to her throat.

In a different life she would have loved to do a fine-arts degree. She had often thought about it over the last five years, but had felt too ashamed to admit to Joseph that she hadn't even completed senior school.

She moved past the garments to the office where Massimo was already speaking in rapid-fire Italian to one of the more senior staff.

She felt a sensation like a sharp pain in her chest when she saw the brilliant whiteness of his smile as he looked down at the woman he was speaking to. Why couldn't he smile at her like that, she wondered. Was there a chance he could resurrect the love he'd had for her five years ago?

He turned and found her looking at him. 'Everything all right, Nikki?'

She nodded. 'Fine, yes…everything's fine…'

'Good,' he said, taking her by the hand. 'Now it is time for lunch. Are you hungry?'

'A little,' she said, lowering her eyes.

He gave her hand an almost imperceptible squeeze. 'Come; you are looking pale and in need of refreshment,' he said, and led her out to the car.

Over a leisurely lunch in a café on a cliff overlooking the sea, Massimo told her some of the island's history, how Sicily was the largest island in the Mediterranean with a rich heritage of art and history.

'Sicily is considered to be the world's first multicultural

society,' he said. 'It has been ruled by Asians, Africans and Europeans, which makes for an eclectic history. You will see thirty centuries of history here, from Greek temples and Roman amphitheatres, Aragonese churches and Arab castles.'

Nikki lapped up the spectacular scenery as they drove back towards Palermo a short time later, the sheer height and drop of some of the cliffs that hugged the coastline breathtaking to say the least.

'We will go first to Cappella Palatina, or Palatine Chapel as it is also known,' Massimo said. 'It contains a wonderful blend of cultures—Byzantine, Norman, Arabic and Sicilian— and has some of the most beautiful mosaics in the world.'

Nikki took his proffered hand a short time later, and looked up in wonder at the wooden ceiling styled into Arab-style stalactites and alveoli dating back to 1143.

They moved on to the cathedral, built in 1184 by the Norman king William II, where Massimo informed her the many renovations over the centuries had resulted in the current neoclassical style. Nikki listened to the deep sound of his voice, the element of pride within it making her realise he was deeply passionate about many things besides business and making money.

He caught her looking at him intently at one point and gave her a rueful smile. 'I am boring you, yes?' he asked.

'No,' she said, a tiny smile pulling at her mouth.

He put a finger to where her lips had lifted slightly, his touch feather-light. 'You nearly smiled,' he said. 'Does that mean you forgive me for being a brute towards you this morning and the other night?'

'We are standing in a cathedral,' she said somewhat wryly. 'I can hardly say no, now, can I?'

His thumb brushed lightly over the surface of her bottom lip. 'I am getting tired of sightseeing. We should have dinner; are you hungry again yet?'

'Not really...' She brought her tongue out just as his thumb came back over her lips, the intimate contact sending sparks of sensation throughout her body.

Their eyes locked for a two-beat pause.

Nikki felt the magnetic pull of his body as hers began to sway towards his. Her heart began to flutter with excitement as his eyes dipped to her mouth, his head moving closer and closer...

The sound of approaching footsteps broke the moment, and with a barely audible sigh he took her hand and led her out to the brilliant sunshine.

Even before they were led to a table in a restaurant a little while later, Nikki could smell the aromas of Sicilian cooking in the air. The hint of wild fennel, mint, almonds, sardines and anchovies all made her mouth start to water.

Massimo ordered some local wine, and when it arrived raised his glass to hers. 'Let us toast to peace while in Italy,' he said. 'I do not want our time here spoilt by pointless bickering.'

She met his eyes across the top of her glass. 'I'm not the one doing the bickering.'

He frowned at her in disapproval. 'That is not helping, Nikki. Come; let us put the past aside for a few days and act like any other couple on holiday.'

She backed down with a sigh and touched her glass against his. 'All right,' she said. 'To peace between us.'

'Good girl,' he said with a smile. 'That did not hurt, did it?'

'Not so far.'

'You do not trust me to keep my promise?' he asked.

Nikki looked at the glass in her hand rather than at his face. 'It is hard for me to trust anyone,' she confessed. 'I guess it comes from my childhood.'

'Tell me about it, *cara*,' he said. 'Was it so very terrible? I know you said you did not want to discuss it, but perhaps it will help to talk of it.'

Her eyes flicked to his before moving away again. 'It doesn't help, Massimo. Talking doesn't change anything.'

Massimo felt his stomach clench as he looked at the shadow of deep sadness in her eyes. 'You were not...' he paused as he searched for the right word '...abused in some way, were you?'

The silence was broken only by the sound of crockery and cutlery being used on the nearby tables, the lively, convivial chatter a stark backdrop to the closed expression on her face.

'Nikki?' he prompted gently.

'Not in the way you mean,' she said at last. 'But there are other ways to make a child's life miserable.'

'*Il mio povero tesoro,*' he said, reaching for her hand.

She looked at him. 'What does that mean?'

He held her look for a long time before he spoke. 'It means I am getting soft where you are concerned, Nikki.'

She looked down at their joined hands and asked softly, 'Is that a good thing or a bad thing?'

He brought her hand up to his mouth and brushed her fingertips with his lips, his eyes locking on hers. 'I guess I will have to wait and see.'

CHAPTER TWELVE

NIKKI hadn't really trusted him to keep his word, but over the next few days he never once mentioned the past. She could feel herself gradually relaxing as each day passed, the hope in her chest gradually unfolding like the petals of a delicate flower each time he smiled at her.

The nights she spent in his arms, his passion for her seemingly increasing as each day passed. She gave herself up to the wild torrent of feelings that coursed through her at the first brush of his lips and the first touch of his tongue. His body surged into hers, his groans of pleasure like music to her ears. She loved the feeling of him losing himself; the total relaxation of his body in her arms made her feel as if she had touched him in a way no one had ever done before. She became increasingly bold with her worship of his body, relishing in the harsh grunts of response that came from deep within him when she pushed him to the brink time and time again.

The last night before they were to leave for Melbourne came all too soon. Nikki hoped the change in location wouldn't sever the atmosphere of friendliness that had grown along with their passion. So many times over the last couple of days she had wanted to tell him of her reasons for marrying Joseph. His gentled attitude towards her made her feel as if she might be able to trust him enough to reveal the dark pain of her past.

But each time she mentally rehearsed the words, her guilt over Jayden's condition would assail her all over again.

As unpredictable and violent as her father had been, she had never imagined that standing up to him that day would have such an outcome. The vision of that afternoon was etched on her brain for ever. The black bats of blame had haunted her ever since, circling her, flapping at her in accusation. 'Your fault, your fault, your fault,' they seemed to say with each beat of their wings inside her head.

She couldn't escape from the torture of it. The thought of talking about it in any detail would surely give her a return of the nightmares that had plagued her in those first harrowing years.

'You are looking very pensive this evening, *cara*,' Massimo commented as their main meal was cleared away. 'Are you not looking forward to returning home tomorrow?'

'Sorry,' she said with a tiny glimmer of a wistful smile. 'I'm not very good company tonight, am I?'

'What are you thinking about?' he asked. 'I have been watching you for the last few minutes. Is something troubling you?'

She toyed with her glass, the movements of her fingers nervous and edgy. Could she do it? Could she trust him with her pain? What if he was repulsed by the thought of having a permanent relationship with a violent criminal's daughter? For what man would want that tainted blood running around the veins of his future offspring?

'Massimo.' She brought her eyes up to meet his, the tip of her tongue snaking out to moisten her lips. 'There's something I have wanted to tell you…'

A flicker of disquiet came and went in his gaze. 'You are pregnant?' he said.

She blinked at him, momentarily knocked off course. 'No, of course not,' she said, blushing slightly.

'We made love without protection over a week ago,' he reminded her.

'So?'

'So one would assume, if you have conceived, then you will not have a period on time,' he said. 'When are you due?'

Oh, God, when *am* I due? Nikki thought in panic. She was hardly regular at the best of times, and with the strain of nursing Joseph over the last few months, and her lower than normal body weight as a result of stress and too many missed meals, she had no idea of the rhythm of her body.

'Nikki?'

'Um…next week,' she said. 'But with all the travelling I might go out of whack. I often do.'

'I think it would be best if you go on the pill when we return,' he said. 'I do not want any little accidents.'

Nikki felt her hopes come crashing down. If he cared anything for her, he would want to continue their relationship indefinitely. The conception of a child would not be seen as a burden but a blessing, an intimate bond like no other. How much worse would it have been if she had told him the truth?

She stripped her expression of emotion as she met his gaze. 'There won't be any little accidents,' she assured him. 'It is not necessary for a woman in this day and age to endure an unwanted pregnancy.'

He frowned at her statement. 'You would have a termination?'

Nikki suddenly realised she had backed herself into a tight corner. 'I have no issue with women having the freedom of choice, but for me personally I would try and find an alternative if I should be in that position.'

'You mean have the child adopted out?' he asked, still frowning.

'You make it sound worse than a termination,' she said with a twisted expression. 'My mother made the biggest mistake of her life by marrying my father because she was pregnant with me. By the time she thought about leaving him, she was pregnant again with my brother. Supporting two little kids when you've had very little in terms of secondary education is not easy, even with the government handouts available both then and now. She lost her confidence under my father's constant belittlement. She became complicit in her own subjugation. In her overburdened and tortured mind, Jayden and I became the enemy instead of our father.'

'So she took her frustration out on you and your brother?'

She gave a little shrug that should have communicated indifference, but in the end didn't. 'Occasionally.'

'But your father was the main perpetrator?'

Her eyes fell away from his, the movements of her hands becoming all the more agitated. 'I really don't like talking about this.'

'I know you do not, Nikki,' he said, reaching for one of her hands and squeezing it gently. 'But do you not see how important it is for me to understand what you have been through?'

'Why is it important?' she asked, her mouth turning down in bitterness. 'I'm nothing to you.'

'That is not true.'

She looked at him, hope inflating like a balloon in her chest. 'W-what are you saying?' she asked.

His dark eyes bored into hers. 'I want to understand you, Nikki. I want to know what secrets you are keeping from me. I feel it every time we are together. You always hold something of yourself back. The only time you do not do so is when we are intimate.'

She shifted her gaze, her mouth twisting ruefully again. 'Yes, well, I don't seem to have any control over that.'

He gave her hand another tiny squeeze. 'Neither do I, *cara mio*,' he said. 'I guess our bodies have a language of their own, mmm?'

Nikki moved her fingers against his hold, her stomach turning over at the realisation of literally being held in the palm of his hand.

'You do not like to be vulnerable, do you, Nikki?' he asked.

'Does anyone?'

'Perhaps not,' he conceded. 'But between lovers it is expected that a certain level of vulnerability and openness is a given.'

'We don't have that sort of relationship.'

'No, but we could have.'

Nikki felt her whole body stall at his words. 'What do you mean?'

He turned her hand over and began to stroke the soft skin of her exposed palm with his thumb. 'I am enjoying this truce we have agreed on,' he said. 'What do you say we continue it for a little bit longer?'

'How long are you talking about?'

'I have not thought about a time frame,' he said. 'We are both enjoying being together, are we not?'

It wasn't as if she could deny it, Nikki thought. She had given him plenty of proof of her satisfaction with their arrangement last night, her body rocking and shuddering beneath the surging weight of his. She could still feel him inside her, those tender muscles responding by contracting every time he looked at her with that dark, smouldering gaze.

'We should get a good night's sleep,' he said as the silence crept towards them. 'Although we do not leave until late in the day tomorrow, I do not want you to be too tired.'

Nikki got to her feet on unsteady legs. 'I'm not the least bit tired,' she said. 'I fell asleep this afternoon on the sun lounger.'

He brought her up close, his body brushing the entire length of hers. 'That is the best news I have heard all day,' he said, pressing a hard, brief kiss to her lips.

She slipped her hand into his as they went to their room, her excitement building with each step. She loved him in this mood; his playfulness made her forget about the reasons they were together. It made her forget about his need for revenge; he was just a man who was seriously attracted to her, wanting to be with her at every opportunity.

'Undress for me,' he commanded as he shut the door of the bedroom with a click.

Even a few nights ago Nikki would have baulked at his request, but with a week or so of sunshine and good food she felt her body had taken on a healthy glow it hadn't experienced in years. Her breasts felt fuller and more feminine, her hips less boyish and angular, and the kiss of the sun had made her pasty skin take on a golden hue that shimmered in the soft light of the bedside lamps.

'What do you want me to take off first?' she asked, with a sultry half smile.

'The top,' he said. 'I want to see your breasts.'

She undid her blouse, button by button, taking her time, sending him looks from beneath her lowered lashes as she gradually revealed herself to him.

'Now go lower,' he said. 'And touch yourself.'

That was harder, but she did it because he made her feel as if she was the most beautiful and desirable woman in the world. She watched as his eyes fed off her, the smooth glide of her hands over her breasts and her lower body making his pupils dilate and his throat move up and down convulsively.

'Come here,' he said roughly.

She stepped forward, her arms going up to loop around his neck, her breasts pushing against his chest. 'Like this?' she asked with another seductive half-smile.

He growled as his mouth connected with hers, his tongue driving through her softly parted lips in search of hers, tangling with it erotically. His hands shaped her breasts, his thumbs rolling over each nipple until he tore his mouth off hers to suckle each one, the pull of his mouth on her sensitive flesh making her shiver all over in reaction.

She felt the bed at the backs of her knees as he walked her backwards, his mouth returning to hers with increasing pressure. She opened her legs to accommodate him, the steely brace of his thighs sending her belly into another quiver of delight. There was barely time for preliminaries, although he managed to grab a condom before he drove into her silky warmth with a harsh groan of satisfaction.

Nikki dug her fingers into his back as he set a hurried pace, the urgency of each of his thrusts thrilling her. She felt tension build and build in every nerve of her body, until all she could think about was that final lift-off where all conscious thought was momentarily suspended.

His first intimate stroke of the tight pearl of her femininity sent her soaring, her whole body feeling as if it had splintered into a thousand tiny pieces.

She felt him come on the tail end of her release, the spasms of her body sending him over the edge. She held him as he rocked against her, her heart feeling so full of love for him she had to bite her tongue in case she said it out loud.

She knew he wouldn't believe it if she told him. He would think she was feigning love in an attempt to achieve financial security for herself.

Massimo lifted his head and looked into her eyes. 'What is that little frown for?' he asked.

Nikki tried to relax her brow. 'Am I frowning?'

He traced a finger over the space between her eyebrows. 'You will get wrinkles if you frown all the time.'

'Smiling is worse,' she said, lifting a finger to outline his top lip. 'You use more muscles to smile than to frown.'

He gave her a teasing smile. 'Did you just make that up?'

'No, I read it somewhere, in a magazine I think,' she said, moving her finger to brush over his bottom lip.

'Ah, but happy people live longer,' he said, capturing her wandering finger and pressing a tiny light-as-air kiss to the end of it. 'A positive outlook on life is a recipe for longevity.'

Her frown came back and her fingers dropped away from his mouth. 'But happiness is not always up to the individual,' she said. 'You can have the most positive outlook in the world, but some circumstances in your life can eventually drag you down.'

'Like your childhood?'

She turned her head away. 'You promised not to mention it again,' she said, her mouth turning down at the edges. 'It's taken me years to put it behind me. I don't want to have to bring it into every conversation we have.'

Massimo felt the aching loneliness of her soul, the sadness in her eyes making his chest feel tight. He couldn't help feeling a little guilty about the way he had forced her back into his life. He had been hell-bent on revenge, not really stopping to think if there was a reasonable explanation for what she had done. Even now he still couldn't think of a single set of circumstances that he would find acceptable for doing what she had, but, as she had said a few days ago, perhaps he hadn't thought deeply enough.

His childhood had been reasonably happy until his mother had deserted his father, but he knew of others who had suffered greatly at the hands of their parents. The newspapers were full of it almost daily—neglect, shaming, abuse both physical and sexual; the cruelty of some adults continually astounded him.

He thought about Nikki's young body being brutalised in some way, for what else had put those haunting shadows in her eyes? She tried to hide it, most particularly when arguing with him. Although she stood her ground with a defiant set to her mouth, he had noticed she never allowed herself to be backed into corners, as if she had already worked out the nearest and quickest escape-route if she ever needed to take it.

It surprised him how much he was affected by her every mood. He liked it when she smiled, and he liked it when she gave herself to him with increasing abandon. He liked the way she kissed him so passionately, her arms flung around his neck as she had done in the past. He hadn't expected his feelings for her to be reawakened in such a way.

Damn it! He didn't want them to be reawakened. He wanted to continue to hate her for betraying him, to make her pay for the heartache she had caused.

She had sold herself to his stepfather, and according to what the lawyer had said she had had numerous affairs during the five years she and Joseph Ferliani had been together.

He had to remember that.

She wasn't to be trusted.

A sneaking suspicion began to lurk at the edges of his mind, and although he hated allowing it purchase he reasoned he had to examine this from all possible angles. What if she was making the stuff about her childhood up? He had heard stories of such things before, a wayward child causing trouble by casting aspersions in order to destroy a parent. Whole families had been torn apart by such specious claims.

What if she had done the same in order to garner sympathy from his stepfather? If so it had certainly worked, as within a few short weeks of working for Joseph Ferliani she had married him.

And now she was doing it to him, reeling in his sympathy for her hard life, in the hope that he would relax his plan for revenge.

'Nikki,' he said turning her head around to face him. 'Where did you grow up?'

Her eyes flared with sudden anger, her hand pulling his away from her face. 'You're not listening to me, Massimo. I told you, I don't want to talk about it.'

He captured her hands and held them above her head as

she bucked and rolled beneath him. 'Stop it, Nikki. It is not such a difficult question, and if you do not tell me then I will have to engage the services of a private investigator to find out for myself. Which would you prefer?'

The fight went right out of her. She lay very still in his hold, her body now limp. 'I grew up in Mount Isa,' she said in a flat, toneless voice.

Massimo knew she was lying. He was starting to recognise the signs now that he had spent time with her. She couldn't hold his gaze, and her face took on a betraying hue of faint colour. 'I can always check that, you know,' he said.

She gave him a defiant look. 'Check it, see if I care. You won't find anything.'

'No, because you did not grow up there, did you?'

She clamped her mouth shut and turned her head away again.

Massimo let out a sigh and got off the bed. 'I am going to have a shower. Do you want to join me?'

She answered by pulling the sheets over her head.

The next morning he joined her at breakfast on the sun-drenched terrace with a frown on his forehead. 'It looks like you are going to get your business-class flight after all, *cara*,' he said as he pulled out the chair to sit down. 'I will not be able to accompany you back to Melbourne as planned. I have some unexpected business to see to. I will have to stay on for another week at the very least.'

Nikki tried not to show her disappointment, and concentrated on pouring him a cup of the delicious coffee Carine had set out just moments earlier. 'It's all right,' she said. 'I have plenty to keep me occupied in Australia.'

He took a quick sip of the coffee before placing it back

down on the table. 'Perhaps you can take a quick trip to Mount Isa to visit your father and brother, eh, Nikki?'

Her cup gave a small rattle against the saucer as she set it back down. 'I don't like the humidity at this time of year,' she said, meticulously avoiding his probing gaze.

'I will try to tie things up here quickly,' he said into the suddenly pulsing silence. 'But I should warn you not to try anything silly while I am away.'

She arched one brow at him. 'You mean such as act like an independent person for a few days?' she asked.

'I meant as in finding yourself another lover to fill in the time,' he said with a warning look. 'Ricardo is under instructions to keep a close eye on you.'

Nikki felt her anger rising like a hot lava-flow inside her. 'Don't judge me by your own despicably low standards,' she tossed back at him. 'I can just imagine what your business here involves.'

His expression darkened. 'I have tried to be patient with you, Nikki,' he said. 'We have had seven days of a truce, and yet you are throwing it away to score points off me.'

'I didn't break the truce—you did. You keep insisting we talk about things I don't want to talk about.'

'You have shared my bed and my body,' he threw back tightly. 'The very least you could do is honour me with the truth.'

'You speak to me of *honour*?' She glared at him. 'You don't even know the meaning of the word! For all I know you're probably bedding a dozen women behind my back as part of your plan for revenge. But I've got news for you—I don't care.'

'Good,' he said as he put his cup down with a sharp crack.

He got to his feet, his dark eyes glittering with barely suppressed anger. 'Enjoy your flight. I will see you in seven days.'

Nikki opened her mouth to fling a bitter retort his way, but stopped when she saw Carine coming out of the door leading to the terrace. The little housekeeper had to step sideways to avoid cannoning into Massimo, who glowered at her on his way past.

She came over to Nikki and set the rolls down, her expression grim. 'Signore Androletti is in a bad mood. I hope it is not because of the phone call he had this morning.'

Nikki picked up her cup with a shaky hand. 'What phone call?'

Carine blew out a breath. 'I should not really tell you, but I do not like that woman,' she said. 'She calls all the time and demands to speak to Signore Androletti.'

'You mean Sabrina Gambari?'

Carine nodded, her mouth pulled tight.

'What did she want?' Nikki asked, trying not to sound too interested.

'She wants to see him, of course,' Carine said. 'She will not take no for an answer.'

Nikki felt a mouthful of coffee come back up into her mouth from her stomach, the acid burn scalding her throat. 'Do you think that's the business he has to see to this morning?' she asked before she could stop herself.

Carine gave her a world-weary look. 'I was hoping it was over between them,' she said. 'When he brought you here I was so certain he would settle down with you, but now he cannot do so.'

Nikki moistened her lips. 'Why is that?' she asked, her throat feeling tight and scratchy.

The young housekeeper bit her lip, glancing back at the villa uncertainly. 'I am not sure I should tell you…'

'It's all right,' Nikki reassured her.

'But you are involved with Signore Androletti,' Carine said. 'I do not want to hurt you.'

Nikki decided to be honest with the young woman. 'Carine, listen to me,' she said. 'I am only a temporary interest of Signore Androletti. He is not in love with me. I have known that from the beginning.'

'But what about your feelings for him?' Carine asked with a concerned frown.

'My feelings are irrelevant,' Nikki said sadly. 'That's also something I've known right from the start.'

Carine took a breath and clutched at the back of the chair Massimo had not long vacated. 'Signorina Gambari is pregnant,' she said. 'I heard one of the villagers talking about it this morning when I was getting the rolls from the bakery.'

Nikki felt her chest tighten to the point of pain. She could scarcely breathe for the weight of it crushing against her chest.

His ex-mistress was having his child.

'That is why he cannot come back to Australia with you,' Carine continued. 'I am certain he is going to marry that woman. It will be expected. The Gambari family will insist on it.'

'But surely that is up to Massimo?' Nikki put in. 'He doesn't strike me as the type to be pushed around.'

'No, but a son and heir is what every Italian man craves,' Carine said. 'Signorina Gambari might not be his first choice for a wife, but she has taken the matter right out of his hands by producing a child for him. He will not allow a child of his to grow up illegitimate.'

'What if it isn't his child?' Nikki asked.

Carine began to clear the table, her expression still grim. 'I guess we will have to wait and see.'

CHAPTER THIRTEEN

NIKKI'S arrival in Melbourne was hampered by heavy fog, which meant the flight had to be redirected to Sydney and wait there for several hours until the airport was reopened.

Ricardo met her in the arrivals hall and transported her to Massimo's house, his glances from time to time as she surreptitiously brushed at her eyes making her wish she had better control over her emotions.

She had desperately hoped Massimo would come back to the villa in time to speak to her before she left, but the hours had dragged past without him returning. It made her realise how little he cared for her to send her back like a parcel, instead of a person with feelings, with hopes and dreams. Her mind filled with images of him with his mistress, perhaps celebrating the news of her pregnancy, planning their wedding and future together.

She clenched her sodden tissue in her hand and gulped back another sob, her tear-washed eyes staring sightlessly out of the window as the rain lashed down outside.

'Signore Androletti has instructed me to drive you wherever you need to go,' Ricardo said as he carried her luggage into the house forty minutes later.

'I know what he said, but I don't need a driver,' Nikki said. 'I prefer to use public transport.'

'You would be wise to do as he says,' Ricardo warned.

She gave him a scathing look as she moved towards the staircase. 'I don't take orders from Signore Androletti.'

'I do not want to lose my job.'

She turned around to look at him. 'If he fires you over me refusing to be chauffeured around then he's even more ruthless and dishonourable than I thought.'

'He is a good man,' Ricardo insisted. 'He will always do the most honourable thing.'

Nikki suppressed an inward sigh as she continued up the stairs. That was the whole reason her heart was breaking all over again. They had missed their chance five years ago, and in spite of all her hopes they were not going to get another one.

It was too late.

The phone was ringing as Nikki came out of the bathroom three days later. 'Hello?'

'Nikki,' Massimo's voice greeted her coolly. 'You took so long to pick up I was beginning to wonder if you had run away.'

'I can hardly do that with your little watchdog on my tail all the time,' she told him resentfully.

He gave a soft chuckle of laughter. 'Ricardo knows which side his bread is buttered,' he said. 'And hopefully so do you.'

'I want to move out,' she said. 'There's no point in continuing this arrangement now.'

There was a momentary pause.

'Are you forgetting the money you owe me?' he asked.

'Are you forgetting the woman you got pregnant?' she shot back.

This time the silence pulsated for endless seconds.

'As far as I know I have not impregnated any woman,' he said. 'Unless, of course, you have some news of your own to tell me.'

Nikki felt a flutter of panic deep in her belly. Her period hadn't arrived, and the tiredness she had assumed was jet-lag had continued regardless of the amount of sleep she'd had.

'Nikki?'

'No, of course not,' she said. 'But I thought—'

'I told you my ex-mistress was determined,' he said before she could finish her sentence. 'But I am not so foolish as to fall for that trick.'

'H-how did you find out it wasn't yours?' she asked.

'I insisted on a paternity test, but in the end it was not necessary, as Sabrina confessed she had been lying about being pregnant.'

'Oh…'

'So that is why I am returning to Melbourne the day after tomorrow,' he said. 'I will expect you to be waiting for me.'

'That's what I am being paid to do,' she said with a barb of bitterness in her tone.

'Yes,' he said. 'You are, and you had better not forget it.'

'You're an arrogant bastard,' she said. 'I should have known that the first time I met you.'

'You sound like you are missing me, *cara*,' he drawled. 'You are spoiling for another fight, mmm?'

Nikki ground her teeth. 'I can't wait to get away from you. I hate you.'

He laughed again. 'You are not going to get away from me until I say so, *cara*. That is the deal, remember?'

Nikki could feel her emotions spilling over again. With

Ricardo following her every move, she hadn't been able to visit Jayden since she'd returned from Sicily. She'd called and the carer on duty had told her he hadn't been well; his fits had increased alarmingly, and he'd had a bad chest infection which wasn't responding to treatment.

'I-I can't do this any more...' she choked. 'I just can't.'

'Nikki.' His tone softened a fraction. 'You are crying?'

'Of course I'm not crying,' she sobbed. 'I n-never cry.'

Massimo released a long-winded sigh. 'I am sorry, Nikki,' he said. 'You are feeling trapped, eh?'

'Y-yes,' she sniffed. 'Ricardo follows me like a shadow. I can't bear it any more. I hate being looked at all the time. I hated it when I was modelling. I can't be myself.'

'Stop crying, Nikki.'

'I-I'm not crying...'

'Yes, you are. I can hear you.'

'Why should you care?' she asked. 'You hate me, re-member?'

'I have not forgotten my feelings for you,' he said after another little pause.

Nikki gave another little sniff. 'I just want this to be over,' she said. 'How much do I owe you now?'

Massimo tightened his resolve. 'I will tell you when I get back,' he said.

'But I need to know now.'

'Why?'

'Because this is not working for us, Massimo,' she said. 'You know it's not. We can pretend to have a truce for a few days, but it doesn't last. There's too much bitterness.'

'You are my mistress now, Nikki. We have a commitment of sorts and I expect you to fulfil your side of it.'

'I don't want to be your—'

'Goodbye, Nikki,' he said. 'I am hanging up.'

'If you hang up I won't be here when you get back,' she threatened.

'If you are not there when I get back I will find you and sue you for the debts you owe,' he countered.

'So either way you win,' she said cuttingly.

'That is right, Nikki. And you had better remember it. You are mine for as long as I want you.'

There was no sign of Ricardo the next day so Nikki could only assume Massimo had called him off. It made her soften towards him, in spite of her anger at the way he was insisting she stay in his life according to the rules he had set down.

She wished she did hate him for it would have made things so much easier, she thought as she made her way to Rosedale House.

Jayden was sleeping when she arrived, his deathly pale face tearing at her heart strings as she sat by his bedside.

The doctor came past just after tea time and asked to speak to her in the office down the hall.

'I am afraid your brother's condition is worsening daily,' Julia Lynch said once Nikki had sat down. 'He's had several grand-mal fits, and in spite of an increased dose of medication it is not controlling them.'

Nikki swallowed back her dread. 'What are you saying?' she asked in a voice hardly above a cracked whisper.

Dr Lynch touched her on the arm, her caramel-brown eyes soft with compassion. 'I don't think he's going to hold on much longer, Nicola. I know we've discussed this earlier, but sometimes it takes a while for it to sink in.'

'I understand...'

'He's been going downhill for quite some time,' Julia continued. 'You did the right thing in getting him in here where the level of care has been consistent, but it's not going to cure him. Nothing was ever going to do that. You do understand that, don't you?'

Nikki nodded, her throat suddenly too tight to speak.

'We are offering him the best level of comfort we can,' Julia said. 'If there is any change we will call you.'

'Thank you.'

'I wish I could offer you more hope,' the doctor said as she got to her feet. 'We see a lot of sad cases in here, but Jayden's is one of the saddest.'

Nikki brushed at her eyes. 'He was such an active kid. He used to surf every morning, he was so good at it. He was bright too, he could have done anything he wanted... anything...'

The doctor gave her shoulder a gentle squeeze. 'Take care of yourself, Nicola.'

'I will...thank you.'

Pia was sitting on the doorstep when Nikki returned, which made her want to cry all over again. She scooped the little cat up in her arms and buried her head against the soft fur. 'How did you know I needed a friend right now?' she asked.

The cat gave her chin a nudge with its head which made a sad smile tug at Nikki's mouth. 'I missed you too, Pia.'

Ricardo appeared briefly to inform her he was going to pick up Massimo from the airport.

'But I thought he said he was coming back tomorrow,' she said with a confused frown.

'He changed his plans,' Ricardo said. 'He lands in just over an hour.'

Nikki couldn't sit still while she waited for Massimo to return. She paced and fidgeted so much Pia stalked out in disgust, and returned to her own home over the back fence.

Nikki heard the car come up the driveway and got to her feet, one of her hands tucking a loose strand of hair behind her ear as Massimo came into the lounge from the foyer.

'Nikki,' he said, his gaze sweeping over her. 'Come here.'

She stood very still, fighting with herself not to dash across the room and throw herself into his arms.

'I said come here.'

'I know what you said, but I'm not coming,' she said with a defiant hitch of her chin.

His mouth tilted in a sardonic smile. 'You are determined to fight me at every opportunity even when it hurts you to do so,' he said.

'What hurts me is being used by you.'

'I am not using you, Nikki. We are both benefiting from this arrangement.'

'How can I trust you to fulfil your side of the agreement?' she asked. 'You say I will be debt free once this is over, but I want proof.'

'All right,' he said after a little silence. 'I'll contact the lawyer in the morning and have something drawn up.'

'I don't want to see Peter Rozzoli. I don't trust him.'

'It seems to me you do not trust anyone,' he said.

'No, that's right, I don't.'

'Is that why you lied to me about growing up in Cairns?'

Nikki felt her throat move up and down but she couldn't get her voice to work.

'I see no reason why you should lie about where you grew up, unless you did something so bad that you have to keep your past a secret,' he said after another stretching silence. 'Is that what this is all about, Nikki? You did something you are ashamed of and want to keep it hidden?'

She drew in a shaky breath when he came closer, her heart thudding erratically when he lifted her chin with one long finger. 'Tell me your little secret, *cara*,' he said.

'T-there's no secret…'

His eyes glinted at her. 'Do I have to tease it out of you?' he asked.

She swallowed as his other hand went to her hip and brought her up against him, pelvis against pelvis, heat against heat, want against want.

He pressed a soft-as-air kiss to the edge of her mouth, making her lips begin to tingle to feel the crushing weight of his.

Her tongue darted out, trying to sweep the sensation away, but before she could close her mouth again his tongue snaked out to flick against hers.

Fire exploded in her belly.

Hot, liquid longing burst between her thighs as his mouth came down hard upon hers, his tongue driving through her already parted lips to mate with hers. She clung to him with desperate fingers curling into the front of his shirt, her mouth feeding hungrily off his, her breathing all over the place as his hands began to wrench wildly at her clothes.

The first touch of his warm palm on her bared breast had her gasping into his mouth as he deepened the kiss. Her body arched towards him, her nipples tight as he left her mouth to suckle each one in turn, his tongue both a torment and a salve as he subjected them to his attention.

She could feel her body singing with pleasure, every nerve end tightening in response to his fevered touch. She pressed herself closer, the hot, hard jut of his body thrilling her to realise he wanted her so badly.

He pushed her backwards towards the sofa, the solid weight of him as they landed in a tangle of arms and legs and half-removed clothes making her sigh with delight as his body nudged hers intimately.

'I want you now,' he groaned as he tugged her skirt upwards, his hands searching for the scrap of lace that barely covered her. 'Right now.'

She lifted her bottom to free her knickers as he gave one last tug on them, her gasp of need deflating her chest when without preamble he surged into her warmth.

She shuddered at the electric-like buzz of him moving inside her, each tender muscle stretching and contracting as the pressure mounted. Her breathing became shallow, her hands clawed at his back, her fingers digging in for purchase as he rode her with rough vigor.

'Look what you do to me,' he growled as he lifted his mouth off hers, his eyes burning into hers. 'You make me lose control.'

'I want you to lose control,' she panted as she lifted her hips to meet the downward thrust of his. 'I want you to want me like I want you.'

'I have always wanted you, Nikki,' he said. 'I do not think it will ever stop, no matter how many times I do this.'

She brought his head back down, her mouth hot and needy on his, her tongue searching for his as her hands held him tightly against her.

He kissed her back with passion that bordered on pain, his

body driving deeply into hers until there was nowhere else to go but paradise. He barely touched her with his fingers and she was there, her high cries of pleasure sounding almost primal to her own ears.

He followed closely, his body stiffening before the final plunge, the pumping thrusts as he spilled himself sending her backwards into the springiness of the sofa.

He lay against her, his breathing still ragged, his lips touching the soft skin of her neck, his words when he spoke tickling her. 'Do not move, Nikki. I want to feel you around me, holding me.'

Nikki let her fingers dance over the smooth skin of his back, her fingertips exploring each knob of his vertebrae, her stomach giving a little kick of lingering pleasure as she felt the moist heat of him between her thighs.

She gave a soft sigh as he brushed his mouth over hers in a soft kiss that was almost tender, and, opening her eyes, searched his face. 'Massimo?'

'What is it, Nikki?' he asked, brushing the hair off her face.

She traced a fingertip over the curve of his upper lip. 'Nothing. I just wanted to make sure I wasn't dreaming…'

He kissed her again, slowly, lingeringly, finally lifting his head to ask, 'Does it seem like a dream to you, *cara*? This thing we share?'

'A bit,' she said, her finger moving to his bottom lip. 'I keep thinking I am going to wake up and it will be over.'

'It is not over yet, Nikki,' he said, kissing her fingertip as it came past. 'Not by a long shot.'

Her eyes came back to his. 'But it will eventually, won't it?'

He frowned as he saw the glint of moisture in her eyes.

'Let's not talk about the future or the past,' he said as he brought his mouth back down to hers. 'Let's just concentrate on the here and now; it is all we have.'

Nikki sighed as his kiss carried her away on another tide of pleasure. He was right, she told herself. They had no future, and the past was too painful to contemplate revisiting.

They had here and now, and that was all.

CHAPTER FOURTEEN

NIKKI woke up to find Massimo lying propped up beside her, his dark gaze fixed on hers.

She began to sit upright, but a wave of nausea suddenly assailed her. She blinked back the white spots from in front of her eyes and flopped back down, her fingertips tingling as the blood drained out of her face.

'Nikki?' he asked, leaning closer. 'What is wrong? Your face is like chalk.'

She swallowed back the rising bile in her throat. 'I don't feel so good…'

'You don't eat enough,' he chided her as he got out of bed and reached for a towel to hitch around his waist. 'I'll bring you some tea and toast.'

'No.' She swallowed again. 'Please…I don't want anything…'

Massimo turned to see her lurch out of the bed and stumble towards the bathroom. 'Nikki?' He stepped on the bed rather than waste time going around it to get to her, but even so she had fallen to her knees in front of the toilet before he could get there.

He winced as she heaved and, kneeling down beside her,

pulled her hair back from her face as she finished. He rinsed a face cloth, gently wiped her face and neck and helped her to her feet. 'I think you should see a doctor,' he said, handing her a fresh towel.

Nikki buried her head in the soft, fragrant towel rather than look at him. 'Yes,' she said weakly. 'I think I will. I've been a bit run down for ages.'

Massimo felt guilt pierce him like a thin, serrated knife. How many times had she ministered to Joseph in the same way or even worse? Long periods of chemotherapy were notorious for making people desperately ill. How had she managed all on her own?

He tucked her hair behind her ear. 'Caring for my stepfather was very difficult, wasn't it, Nikki?'

She nodded, her face still hidden in the towel.

He let out a sigh and gently held her against him. 'He was lucky to have you.'

Nikki lifted her head to look at him. 'He was a good man, Massimo,' she said. 'I know you hated him, but he really tried to make amends for what he did.'

He put her from him, his expression losing its earlier softness. 'I have to go to the office,' he said. 'Will you be all right, or shall I call a doctor to come to the house?'

'I'll see my own doctor,' she said. 'But I'm sure it's nothing serious. I'm probably still a bit jet-lagged.'

He stood for a moment in the doorway, his eyes holding hers. 'Do you think there is a chance you could be pregnant?' he asked.

'No.'

'You seem rather definite about that,' he observed.

'I am,' she said, hoping he couldn't see the lie for what it was.

He held her gaze for another three beats before pushing himself away from the door. 'Do not bother to cook dinner tonight,' he said. 'We are dining out—that is, if you feel well enough to do so.'

'I'll be fine,' she said. 'Where are we going?'

'There is a dinner-dance being held to raise funds for one of the charities I support.'

She looked at him in surprise. 'You support a charity?'

He gave her an arched-brow look. 'You do not think I am a charitable person, *cara*?'

She nibbled at her bottom lip, her eyes falling away from his. 'I haven't really thought about it.'

'I have been very charitable towards you, have I not?' he asked. 'I could have taken legal action against you, but instead I gave you a chance to work off the debt.'

She brought her eyes back to his, an accusing glitter shining in their depths. 'Yes, by using me as a sex slave. That's hardly what I'd call charitable behaviour.'

'I am not using you in any such manner. Each time we have made love it has been your choice just as much as mine.'

'We do not make love,' she said. 'We have sex.'

'It amounts to the same thing, Nikki, no matter what term you use.'

She clenched her fists by her sides. 'It's not the same thing at all! You don't love me.'

'I do not *want* to love you,' he threw back angrily.

She blinked at him for a second or two. 'You mean…you mean you're *fighting* it?' she asked.

He raked a hand through his hair. 'I am going to work. Be ready by seven.'

She took a step towards him. 'Massimo?'

'Leave it, Nikki,' he dismissed her coldly. 'You killed my love for you five years ago. I cannot switch it back on again even if I wanted to.'

Nikki let out a ragged breath as the door snapped shut on his exit. She turned and looked at her reflection in the mirror, and grimaced. She had ten hours to get ready for this evening and she was going to need each and every one of them.

The doctor's surgery was crowded, which meant Nikki had to wait much longer than normal, which did nothing to settle her nerves. She flicked through the magazines on the table in the waiting room, every now and again finding a photograph of herself in one of the Ferliani advertisements. It was almost surreal, looking at that carefully constructed pose, the smoky made-up eyes, the lush painted curve of her lips, the sexy drape of fabric over her too-slim frame, the creamy perfection of her skin and the silky gloss of her long blonde hair so far away from what she was currently feeling. It was like looking at a stranger.

She looked up when her name was called and followed the doctor into the surgery, taking the chair opposite.

'It's been a while since you were in,' Dr Harris said, looking at her notes. 'What can I do for you, Nikki?'

Nikki decided to come straight to the point. 'I think I might be pregnant.'

Tracey Harris didn't bat an eyelid. 'Have you missed a period?'

'I'm not sure. I haven't been regular for months, but I have some of the symptoms.'

'I'll send off some blood to run a few tests, pregnancy included,' Tracey said. 'I can pull a few strings at the pathology lab. The results will be in by late this afternoon.'

'Thank you.'

Nikki spent the rest of the day with Jayden who, though awake this time, was listless and pale. She tried feeding him at lunch time but he seemed uninterested, and even when she wheeled him outside for some fresh air he screwed up his face, as if the watery sunlight was too bright for his eyes.

She left Rosedale House with a heavy heart, her grief and guilt consuming her all over again at what her brother had suffered on her behalf.

Her mobile rang just as she was coming up the driveway of Massimo's house and she took it out of her bag, her heart chugging unevenly when she saw Dr Harris's number flash up on the screen.

'Nikki, I have the results of your test,' Tracey Harris said.

Nikki held her breath. 'Yes?'

'It's positive,' the doctor said. 'You are pregnant.'

'Oh.'

'I'd like to see you again as soon as you can arrange an appointment,' Tracey went on. 'You are slightly anaemic, and there are some supplements we recommend you take during pregnancy—that is, if you wish to continue with it.'

'Of course I want to continue with it,' Nikki said.

'Sorry, I wasn't sure,' Tracey said. 'We didn't get around to discussing it this morning.'

'I'll call the receptionist in the morning and make an appointment,' Nikki said. 'Thank you for speeding up the results.'

'That's fine, Nikki. Have plenty of rest until I see you again.'

'I will…' she said, and ended the call.

* * *

Nikki dressed in a long, silvery Ferliani ball gown, the slight train on the back like a mermaid's tail, the silky fabric clinging lovingly to every slight curve of her body. She scooped her hair up high on her head, leaving trailing tendrils either side of her face. Dangling diamond earrings hung from her ears, and a sparkling matching pendant nestled in the shadow of her cleavage.

She put her hand on her flat tummy, and felt a quiver of nervousness rush through her at the thought of telling Massimo her news. She could wait for a few more weeks, hoping he might begin to feel something for her again, but she didn't like her chances. It would be better to get it over with, to deal with it head-on instead of drawing it out unnecessarily.

She waited for him in the lounge, her fingers gripping her evening purse until they ached, her stomach churning with anguish as each minute dragged by.

'I am sorry,' Ricardo said as he came into the room. 'Signore Androletti has instructed me to drive you to the function. He has been held up in a meeting. He will meet you there.'

Nikki got to her feet, her legs feeling like wet cotton-wool as the stores of adrenalin leached out of her. 'Thank you, Ricardo. I am ready to leave now.'

The hotel ball room was aglow with sparkling chandeliers and balloons, the banner of the underprivileged-children's charity hanging from one side of the stage to the other. Nikki stared at it for a long time, hardly aware of the buzz of people around her.

'Mrs Ferliani?' A photographer jostled closer.

Nikki was vaguely aware of smiling mechanically for the

camera, but the smile froze on her face when she saw a young woman enter the ball room on Massimo's arm. He was smiling down at her fondly, his eyes so soft with affection it tore at Nikki's heart like long, sharp claws. She felt nausea rise like acid in her throat, and her legs started to wobble beneath her.

'Mrs Ferliani.' A journalist pushed past a knot of people to get to her. 'Is it true you are no longer the face of Ferliani, that Abriana Cavello is taking your place?'

'It is true that I have terminated my contract with Ferliani Fashions—yes,' she answered stiffly.

'Have you met Miss Cavello?' the journalist asked.

'No, not as yet.'

'Are you aware of the rumours circulating about Massimo Androletti's relationship with Miss Cavello?' he asked.

Nikki gave him a cool smile. 'I make it a habit not to listen or even respond to rumours,' she said. 'In any case, they are rarely accurate.'

'How would you describe your current relationship with Mr Androletti?' he asked. 'Are you still living with him?'

'I have no further comment to make,' she said, and turned away to make her way to the powder room.

She locked herself into one of the cubicles and took some steadying breaths, her stomach still threatening to misbehave.

She heard the door of the powder room being pushed open, and the sound of female voices chatting over the basins as lipstick was reapplied.

'Looks like Massimo Androletti has traded in yet another lover,' one woman said. 'I thought he was seeing Nikki Ferliani.'

'He was, but I heard he's finishing with her,' the other woman answered. 'Off with the old and on with the new.'

'Nikki Ferliani is only twenty-four. That's hardly *old*.'

'I know, but you know what these rich playboys are like,' the first woman said. 'They can have anyone they like. Mind you, I think the Ferliani woman is a bit of a user herself. Fancy marrying a man old enough to be her father. Yuck. It makes my flesh crawl just thinking about it.'

'It's amazing what some people will do for money,' the other woman replied as the door opened and closed as they left.

Nikki got unsteadily to her feet and made her way back to the ball room, her face feeling tight as she searched the room for Massimo. She found him to the right of the ball room, chatting with a group of people, Abriana Cavello still hanging off his arm. His eyes collided with hers, and he bent his head to say something to the young woman before he came over to Nikki.

'Nikki, I have been waiting for you to arrive,' he said. 'There is someone I would like you to meet.'

She gave him a filthy look. 'I'm not interested in meeting your new mistress,' she bit out. 'I'm leaving.'

He took her by the arm and led her, out of earshot of the tables they were standing alongside, to the bar outside the ball room.

He waited until they were both seated away from the other guests before he announced, 'Abriana is not my mistress.'

She glared at him. 'You expect me to believe that?'

'I expect you to remember the agreement we made,' he returned.

'I'm not doing it any more,' she said, grey-blue sparks of defiance firing in her eyes. 'I don't care if you sue me.'

His eyes gleamed as they held hers. 'You are calling my bluff, mmm? Testing me to see if I will follow through on my threats.'

Nikki felt close to tears. 'If you sue me then you will be hurting your own flesh and blood,' she said.

He frowned as he looked at her. 'What do you mean?'

She moistened her lips with her tongue, her eyes flicking sideways to see if anyone was listening. 'I'm pregnant.'

It was a long time before he spoke.

'I suppose it would be impolitic of me to ask if it is mine?'

'It would be very cruel of you to do that,' she said, her eyes taking on a wounded look. 'But if you want a test done to establish paternity then I will agree to it.'

He let another silence pass for several moments.

'What have you decided to do?' he asked.

'I haven't had time to think about it,' she said, fidgeting with the clasp on her purse. 'I just thought you should know.'

'Thank you for telling me.'

Nikki searched his face, but his expression was almost impossible to read. 'I didn't mean for this to happen,' she said. 'You have to believe that, Massimo.'

'What is it you want from me, Nikki?'

'W-what do you mean?'

'That was your plan, wasn't it, Nikki?' he asked. 'You orchestrated it very well, I have to admit—playing cool and coy to begin with, ramping up my desire for you to such a degree I made love to you without protection. It was a clever tactic and timed to perfection.'

She opened and closed her mouth, trying to get her voice to work. 'I did no such thing!' she insisted.

'Do not play me for a fool,' he ground out. 'You forget, I have already been down this road recently. I am not going to believe you are carrying my child until I see evidence of it.'

She sent him a glittering glare. 'I have the test results at your house.'

He gave a little snort. 'That is not going to be good enough for me. I will want to see my DNA on the printout as well.'

'You are a heartless bastard,' she spat at him furiously. 'I wish I had never told you. I should have kept it a secret to punish you.'

'That is exactly the sort of thing a woman like you would do, isn't it, Nikki?' he asked in a snide tone. 'You love your little secrets. But, you forget, I have the means to uncover them. What will you do then, I wonder?'

Nikki stared at him as the fear chugged through her veins. She told herself it didn't matter any more. Jayden wasn't going to live much longer, so the issue of providing for him would be removed. Her own shame she could deal with. She didn't intend being in the public eye any more, so it wouldn't matter in the least. And, as for any future with Massimo, well, that was a dream turned to dust like most of her others.

'I am not going to offer you marriage,' he said into the tight silence. 'I will help you financially once it is established that the baby is actually mine.'

Nikki got to her feet in one rigid movement. 'Please don't bother. I can manage on my own. If I have to live on the streets I will do it rather than accept a single cent from you.' She swung away and stalked out of the bar, desperately trying not to cry until she was alone.

'Would you like a drink, sir?' a hovering waiter asked Massimo.

Massimo turned to look at the waiter and frowned. 'What?'

The waiter indicated the bar behind him and repeated his question.

'Yes,' Massimo said as he saw Nikki climb into a cab on the lower level. 'And you had better make it a double.'

Nikki stared at the passing streets with unseeing eyes, her heart feeling as if it had been crushed beneath a heavy weight. Pain filled her chest until she could hardly breathe, her throat burned and her eyes streamed.

She hadn't been expecting him to be happy about her news, but neither had she expected him to be so cold and clinical about it. During that wonderful week in Sicily she had felt such a change in him. She had hoped he was starting to care something for her again; she had even felt as if she was starting to trust him enough to tell him about Jayden. But then there had been the issue of his ex-mistress, which had ruined the atmosphere of peace between them.

Although, when she recalled his gorgeous and very young new lover standing beside him this evening, she had no choice but to assume he had only been using her as a temporary fill-in.

As revenges went, it was up there with the best. There was no better way to drive the nail home than have a quick fling with her and walk away, as he felt she had done to him five years ago.

Nikki opened her purse to get another tissue, and saw that there was a message icon on her mobile. She had turned it to silent when she had gone to meet Massimo at the dinner, but obviously someone had been trying to reach her. She looked down at the received-calls list and her stomach gave a sudden lurch. She dialled the message service, her heart thumping as she listened to someone who identified themselves as Jayden's doctor in Intensive Care, the short but urgent message sending another wave of panic and dread through her.

She put the phone away with shaking fingers and leaned forward to speak to the cab driver. 'I'm sorry, could I change my destination to the Western General Hospital? And please hurry; it's an emergency.'

'How long has he been like this?' Nikki asked Dr Cardle in Intensive Care.

'He was brought in a couple of hours ago,' the doctor said. 'Rosedale House tried to contact you earlier. He had a fit at tea time, but came out of it reasonably well. However, he had another one as they were putting him to bed. He fell and hit his head and has been in a coma ever since.'

Nikki bit the inside of her cheek as she looked at her broken brother hooked up to various machines, his tall, thin frame taking up so little space in the bed.

'I'm sorry to have to tell you this,' the doctor said gently. 'But there has been an intracranial bleed that has caused even more damage to his brain. There is no possible hope of recovery.'

Nikki brushed at her eyes and faced the doctor. 'Can he breathe on his own?'

David Cardle shook his head. 'The ventilator is keeping him alive. Dr Lynch thought you would want to be with him when it is turned off.'

Nikki swallowed. 'How long can I have with him?' she asked.

The doctor touched her on the shoulder. 'You can have as

long as you want,' he said. 'Is there anyone you would like to call to be with you? I noticed you are nominated as the next of kin, but is there anyone else who could support you right now?'

Nikki shook her head. 'No, there's no one I want with me right now,' she said, trying to control the tremble of her bottom lip.

'I will be in the office if you need anything,' he said.

'Thank you...'

Nikki sat by her brother's bed for seven hours. She stroked his hand, kissed each of his fingers, his nose, his forehead and each of his cheeks, telling him how much she loved him, how sorry she was, how she would give anything to change places with him.

At three minutes to two in the morning, before the ventilator was switched off, Jayden Bradley Jenkins passed away with his sister's hand in his.

Nikki walked out of the hospital a few hours later just as the sun was coming up on a new day. She walked to the tram stop in an invisible bubble of grief that even the chill wind couldn't penetrate.

The tram was crowded with the first wave of early-morning commuters, but as she jostled to find a position Nikki realised she had never felt more acutely alone in her life.

CHAPTER FIFTEEN

'I THINK you should see this,' Abriana Cavello said, pushing the morning paper towards her godfather a few days later.

Massimo put down his coffee and stared at the photographs, his brow furrowing as he read the article below. His throat went up and down, and his gut tightened the more he read.

'The funeral is today,' Abriana said into the silence. 'It's supposedly private, but I think you should go.'

He scraped a hand through his hair, still staring at the grainy police-photo of Nikki's father. He had heard of the brutal murder of Kaylene Jenkins in Perth several years ago. It had shocked the nation that a husband could be so chillingly sadistic. He had turned the axe he had used on his wife on his sixteen-year-old daughter Nicola, but she had managed to escape the first blow. The younger brother Jayden had tried to protect her and had suffered horrendous head injuries.

'Yes,' Massimo said, looking up at Abriana, swallowing convulsively again. 'Yes… I will go.'

'Do you want me to organise some flowers?' she asked.

'No,' he said, rubbing at his face for a moment. 'I will do that.'

'Would you like me to come with you, Uncle Mass?'

He gave her a grim look. 'No.'

'You didn't know about this, did you?' she asked.

He shook his head, his eyes taking on a bleak dullness.

Abriana looked back at the paper, still open on his desk. 'If I came from that sort of background I would want to keep it a secret too,' she said. 'But I wonder how the press found out.'

He got to his feet and walked to the window to look down at the city below. Guilt knifed through him. *He* had probably been responsible for the leak, given that he'd had a private investigator searching for information on her whereabouts. Tony Carpenter had finally located her, staying at a small hotel in the suburbs, but he hadn't gone to see her. Massimo had read a small interview in the paper, in which she'd been quoted as saying she had hooked up with someone else and was extremely happy. He had thrown the paper down in disgust, his anger towards her so intense he hadn't trusted himself to confront her personally.

'I don't know,' he said heavily. 'Maybe someone at the hospital recognised her or something.'

'Uncle Mass?'

'Mmm?' he answered absently, his mind filling with images of Nikki sitting alone by her brother's bedside, watching his last breaths of life leave his body.

'Finding out about her background hasn't changed the way you feel about her, has it?'

He slowly turned around to look at her. 'What do you mean?'

'I mean, you still love her, don't you?' she asked. 'It's not her fault she had an awful father. Lots of people have terrible parents, and even brothers and sisters. A friend of mine has a brother who is in jail for robbing a service station. She's only told me; not even her boyfriend knows about it. But you wouldn't hold something like that against Nikki, would you?'

He came over and, taking her head in his hands, kissed her on the forehead. 'Thank you, Abby.'

She wrinkled her nose at him. 'What did I do?'

'You made me realise what an absolute idiot I have been,' he said. 'No wonder she didn't tell me. I am a blind, stupid fool for not realising she had something like this to hide. She hinted at it a couple of times. God, I have probably ruined my chances of ever repairing the damage, but I am going to do my best to try.'

Nikki sat in the chapel waiting for the chaplain to arrive, her brother's coffin in front of her adorned with white flowers, the fragrance of lilies lingering in the air.

She had never been a particularly religious person, God had not seemed to be listening any of the times she had prayed for help. But somehow in the chapel she drew a small measure of comfort from the sweet cadences of the hymns playing softly in the background.

The chaplain appeared at the same time as someone entered the pew and sat down beside her. Nikki turned her head, her eyes widening as she encountered Massimo's dark-brown gaze.

'Nikki,' he said, reaching for her hand.

Her heart began to race as his fingers curled around hers, the tenderness in his eyes making hers glisten with tears, but she didn't have a chance to speak as just then the chaplain began the short but meaningful service.

Several journalists surged towards them as they left the crematorium a little while later but Massimo herded them off with a curt dismissal. Nikki felt the strong protection of his arms about her waist, and felt safe for the first time in more years than she could remember.

Massimo led her to his car, instructing Ricardo to drive them to his house before helping Nikki inside the vehicle, joining her on the seat and taking her hand in his again.

'I do not know where to begin,' he said, stroking the back of her hand with his thumb. 'When I saw that article in the paper…' He swallowed and continued hollowly, 'I cannot tell you how I felt. I have treated you unforgiveably. Can you find it in your heart to forgive me for my ignorance and arrogance and unspeakable cruelty?'

Nikki looked at him with eyes still red and swollen. 'I should have told you…I wanted to so many times…'

'I can imagine why you did not,' he said in harsh self-recrimination. 'I had not shown an ounce of compassion towards you. I talked of having my revenge, forcing you into a relationship no one of your nature would have been ready for. You had just buried your husband. My opinion of you was so misguided I did not think you capable of having any feelings for him or anyone. It was all about money, or so I thought.'

'It was all about money,' she said, staring down at their linked hands.

He brought her chin up. 'Yes, but not money for you—money for your brother.'

'Yes.'

'*L'oh il mio povero tesoro piccolo,*' he said. 'How you must have suffered.'

'It's over now,' she said on the tail-end of a ragged sigh.

'Jayden's at peace finally. I hated seeing him like that. He had been such an active and bright, intelligent kid. I will never forgive myself for what happened to him.'

'It was not your fault, *cara*.'

She looked at him with such aching sadness in her eyes, Massimo felt his chest tighten unbearably.

'It *was* my fault,' she said. 'I should have known something was wrong that day. I was usually so good at judging my father's moods. But he had killed my mother, Massimo.' She paused and when she spoke again her voice wavered. 'Killed her that afternoon, while Jayden and I were at school. I didn't know. He was so argumentative and belligerent, so I stood up to him, determined not to be reduced to the quivering wreck my mother had become. I didn't realise Jayden had heard us arguing. He was supposed to be at a friend's house that afternoon, but I later found out the friend had been sick so he had come home instead.'

Massimo pulled her into his arms, caressing the silky tresses of her hair as she told him the rest in fits and starts. He had tears in his eyes by the time she finished. She had been through hell and back, fighting for survival for most of her life.

Her courage astounded him. She had forged a career for herself, done everything in her power to protect the person she loved and believed she had let down.

He led her into the house a few minutes later and, pouring her a drink, joined her on the sofa, drawing her close. 'I can understand now why you were so derisive of my attitude towards my stepfather,' he said. 'My behaviour must have seemed so petty compared to your situation.'

'It wasn't petty—just a little pointless,' she said. 'Joseph had suffered enough. If you had seen him those last few weeks…'

He brought her hand up to his mouth and kissed it tenderly. 'You are the most compassionate person I have ever known. I thought so that first time we met. I was drawn to you as soon as you walked into the bar. It was like you were my other half, the missing half I had been searching for.'

'I'm so sorry I hurt you back then.'

He pushed her lips closed with his finger. 'No, I am the one who should be apologising. I am no doubt going to be doing it for the rest of our lives.'

She blinked at him. 'You want me to…?'

'Lo sposerete il mio tesoro?' he asked with a melting smile.

She smiled back, her eyes lighting up with joy. 'Are you asking me to marry you?'

'Yes, Nikki. I love you. I thought I no longer did, but my goddaughter Abriana made me realise I had never really stopped.'

Nikki gaped at him. *'Your goddaughter?'*

'Yes,' he said with a sheepish look. 'I promised her parents I would help her get into modelling. The press has made a bit of an issue out of us, but you know what they're like—never interested in the truth.'

'That night of the dinner when I saw you come in with her I was so hurt that you seemed to have moved on so quickly,' she said. 'When a journalist approached me the other day I told them I was seeing someone, but of course I wasn't. There has never been anyone but you.'

He hugged her close, his arms around tight to the point of crushing. 'I can never forgive myself for hurting you. I am ashamed of how I treated you when you told me about the baby.'

'I understand,' she said into his chest. 'It must have been hard for you, hearing it so soon after Sabrina's claims.'

He pulled back to look at her. 'I cannot forgive myself for uncovering your past the way I did.'

'What do you mean?'

He took a deep swallow. 'When I returned to the house the evening of the dinner I was sure you would be there waiting for me. I was convinced you would not leave without a large payout. But you were not there. You had not even taken a single article of clothing or your toiletries with you. I sent a private investigator in search of you. He phoned me the next day to say he had found you in a cheap hotel. But I cannot help thinking perhaps he leaked something to the press about you, although he said nothing to me of your background.'

'It wasn't anything you did,' she said. 'One of the nurses at the hospital recognised me from when I was living in Perth. I have spent the last eight years dreading someone recognising the girl I was back then—but, there you go, not even make-up and expensive clothes can hide who you really are.'

'I can understand why you wanted to keep that part of your life a secret, *cara*,' he said. 'But it makes no difference to me. You are still the sweetest, most adorable woman I have ever met.'

Tears shone in her eyes. 'You mean if I had told you all those years ago you wouldn't have run a mile?'

He brushed at her tears with his thumbs as he cupped her face in his hands. 'I would have done everything in my power to help you get your brother into the care he needed.'

She compressed her lips, her throat moving up and down

as she tried to control her emotions. 'I should have told you. Oh God…I should have told you…'

'Do not torture yourself,' he said. 'It is in the past, and besides you were a wonderful support to my stepfather. If he went to his deathbed a better man then surely it was worth the sacrifice of those five years.'

'I didn't sleep with him, Massimo. I need you to believe me.'

'I do believe you, Nikki,' he said. 'And I have also terminated all dealings with Peter Rozzoli. I had my financial people delve a little into his background. You were right about him. He has been siphoning off funds from Ferliani Fashions for the past year.'

'Poor Joseph.' Nikki said. 'I wonder if he knew…'

'To tell you the truth I was quite surprised when he called me in those months before he died,' Massimo said. 'I have been wondering lately if he did so in order to provide for you.'

She looked at him in puzzlement. 'But he knew you hated me for what I had done.'

'Yes, but he also knew I had not married anyone else,' he reminded her. 'He must have realised I still had feelings for you, otherwise he would not have offered me everything the way he did. But you still have not answered my question, *cara*. Are you going to give me a second chance?'

She touched the side of his face with the softness of her hand, her expression full of wonder that the heartache of the past had finally gone. 'Yes, I am,' she said. 'For remember I said five years ago if we were really meant to be together we would get another chance?'

He covered her hand with his and brought it to his heart. 'I remember, Nikki. This is our time now. We have had to both work for it in our separate ways, but it will be all the sweeter for the waiting.'

'You know something, Massimo?' she said, snuggling up to him. 'I think you are right.'

was. They'll co-operate in every inch will be all the longer

for the waiting.'

'You know what this means?' Massimo said straightfied in

satisfaction. 'They don't—'

EPILOGUE

'WHICH do you like best?' Massimo asked as he leafed through their wedding photos with Nikki a few weeks later.

Nikki peered over his shoulder, pressing a soft kiss to the side of his neck. 'I don't know,' she said, nibbling on his ear. 'I kind of like the one where you're kissing me with the sunset in the background.'

He shivered as her tongue snaked into his ear. 'I like that too.'

'What about this?' she asked, raining hot little kisses all over his face. 'Do you like that too?'

He laughed and tugged her onto his lap, holding her against his hardness. 'You are a minx,' he said. 'I thought you were supposed to be resting each day. Isn't that what pregnant women are supposed to do?'

She pouted at him playfully. 'It's no fun resting on my own,' she said. 'Besides, you're the reason I can't fit into my jeans any more. I think it's only fair you should entertain me when I'm bored.'

He kissed her lingeringly, the sweet taste of her thrilling him all over again. He had not realised how deeply he could love until now. His child lay in her womb, its tiny limbs growing day by day just like his love for her. Each day brought him new awareness of her beauty and grace, her ready forgiveness for the way he had treated her totally humbling him.

The pain of her past was gradually fading. He had stood by her side on a lonely Victorian beach as she had cast her brother's ashes into the rolling waves, tears falling from her eyes as she'd told him how Jayden had been locked away for too long in a body that no longer worked, so it was only fair that he was free to swim and surf as he used to do.

He had felt a lump come to his throat as she'd lifted her face to the salty air, her eyes closing as the sun came out from between the clouds to shine on the water…

'So, how about it, darling?' she asked, pressing a soft kiss to each of his eyelids. 'Are you going to take me to bed and entertain me?'

There was a miaow from the doorway, and Massimo and Nikki both turned their heads in surprise and delight.

'*Pia!*' Nikki hopped off Massimo's lap and scooped up the wasted little body. 'Where on earth have you been? You're so thin! We thought you must have been run over or something. Mrs Lockwood told us you haven't been home for almost two weeks.'

Massimo gave the little black head a gentle stroke. 'Naughty little Pia, you had us so worried. Have you been getting up to mischief?'

The little cat blinked at him guilelessly before leaping from Nikki's arms to saunter to the door leading back out to the garden.

Massimo exchanged a quick glance with Nikki. 'Do you think she is trying to tell us something?' he asked.

Nikki took his hand and tugged him towards the door.
'Come on.'

A few minutes later they stood gazing down at four little
squirming, silky black bodies, hidden away in a corner of the
garden shed, their tiny eyes still glued shut.

'Do you think she's told the father yet?' Nikki whispered
as she squeezed Massimo's hand.

He looked down at her, tears in his eyes as he drew her
closer. 'I certainly hope so,' he said. 'For there can be no
greater thing in life than having the woman you love bear your
children.'

She smiled up at him, her heart swelling to twice its size
as she saw his love for her shining in his eyes. 'Do you think
we could keep one for our baby?' she asked.

'A boy or a girl?'

She rolled her lips together for a moment. 'I don't know,
do you think it matters?'

'What about one of each?' he suggested.

Her eyes went wide. 'You want *two*?'

He pulled her into his arms and breathed in the sweet, fresh
fragrance of her hair. 'I want it all, Nikki. Two kids, two
kittens and you.'

'There's only one of me,' she said, her eyes dancing with
happiness as she gazed up at him. 'Is that going to be
enough for you?'

He lifted her in his arms and carried her back towards the
house. 'More than enough,' he said, and kicked the door shut
with his foot.

NIGHTS *of* PASSION

One night is never enough!

**These guys know what they want
and how they're going to get it!**

UNTAMED BILLIONAIRE, UNDRESSED VIRGIN
by **Anna Cleary**

Inexperienced Sophy has fallen for dark and
dangerous Connor O'Brien. Though the bad boy
has vowed never to commit, after taking Sophy's
innocence is he still able to walk away?

Book #2826

Available May 2009

Don't miss any of these hot stories, where sparky
romance and sizzling passion are guaranteed!

REQUEST YOUR FREE BOOKS!

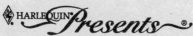

2 FREE NOVELS
PLUS 2
FREE GIFTS!

HP09

HARLEQUIN *Presents*

The **LEOPARDI BROTHERS**

*Sicilian by name…scandalous,
scorching and seductive by nature!*

THE SICILIAN
BOSS'S MISTRESS
by **Penny Jordan**

When billionaire Alessandro Leopardi finds
Leonora piloting his private jet, he's outraged!
So he decides he'll take her for one night. But then
he realizes one night may not be enough….

Book #2819

Available May 2009

Look out for the final story
in this Penny Jordan trilogy,

THE SICILIAN'S BABY BARGAIN,
available in June.

I ♥ HARLEQUIN® *Presents*

BROUGHT TO YOU BY FANS OF HARLEQUIN PRESENTS.

We are its editors and authors and biggest fans—and we'd love to hear from YOU!

Subscribe today to our online blog at
www.iheartpresents.com